Dancing Nightly in the Tavern

Dancing Nightly in the Tavern

stories by
Mark Anthony Jarman

BRINDLE & GLASS

Originally published in 1984 by Press Porcépic Ltd.

Library and Archives Canada Cataloguing in Publication

Jarman, Mark Anthony, 1955-
Dancing nightly in the tavern : stories / by Mark Anthony Jarman. — 2nd ed.
First published: Toronto : Press Porcépic, 1984.
ISBN 978-1-897142-22-6
I. Title.
PS8569.A6D3 2007 C813'.54 C2007-900230-7

Cover image: istockphoto.com
Author photo: Brian Atkinson

The Canada Council for the Arts | Le Conseil des Arts du Canada

Brindle & Glass is pleased to thank the Canada Council for the Arts and the Alberta Foundation for the Arts for their contributions to our publishing program.

Brindle & Glass is committed to protecting the environment and to the responsible use of natural resources. This book is printed on 100% post-consumer recycled and ancient-forest-friendly paper. For more information, please visit www.oldgrowthfree.com.

Brindle & Glass Publishing
www.brindleandglass.com

1 2 3 4 5 10 09 08 07

PRINTED AND BOUND IN CANADA

For Mom and Dad, and Sharon.

Contents

Introduction

Mark Anthony Jarman published this, his first book, in 1984. Twenty-two years ago now. He published it at a time when such short story writers as W.P. Kinsella and W.D. Valgardson were much in vogue. It is not surprising, then, that not much attention was paid. Jarman was not particularly interested in nationalism or regionalism or racial minorities. It would be rather difficult to extract from his stories any moral certainties or comforts. He was not interested in what political claptrap habitually describes as "telling our own stories."

Jarman's not your man for pablum.

His characters want something but don't know what.

> Ray hasn't eaten, has a vision of himself being rolled somewhere, caught with others in the Depression, a post office mural, a Hopper painting in the USA. *Think positively*, Ray counsels himself. *As what we came for*

> *eludes us, so we will replace it. At the food bank there is cheese. Hot coffee and three-bean salad in those cheery church basements. . . .*
>
> This is not the fucking Depression. I will not line up for their handouts, gnaw the bureaucrats' cheddar. There is a bone stuck in my throat. I want, I don't know, something.

Right from the start, Jarman went for the jugular of language. A contemporaneous review of *Dancing Nightly* suggested that Jarman might have been influenced by Jack Kerouac, but this observation is more true of the characters' wallowing in alcohol and drugs than it is of stylistic influence. Kerouac is a rather flabby writer; Jarman is madly fierce. He reminds me less of Kerouac than of the Cormac McCarthy of *Blood Meridian*.

Jarman's landscapes are mythic landscapes of the mind—a mind drunk or drugged with hopelessness. His cities are visions of violence and madness and remind me of Nathaniel West's *Day of the Locust.* His prose is not the delicate register of sociological markers or the accumulation of realist detail for its own sake. His is a prose of apocalyptic incantation.

Here are Jankovitch and Ironchild on the road:

> . . . swinging hard across the blue plains and raggedy-ass cottonwood, the endless flight through pale aspens and truck stop botulism, K-Mart snakeskin cowboy boots, cheating songs, box elders. This is just after the grain elevator blew over to Missouri: burned for days and they couldn't get at the bodies. In the blind pigs

> and roadhouses, lizards cringe under the crashing rain of Wurlitzers and chicken bones.

That is the Jarman voice.

For which we should give thanks.

And while Mark Jarman was blowing and honking and screaming these fervent tenor solos, academe ignored him and placidly munched away on Marian Engel.

Some reviewers have described Jarman's characters as "blue collar," but the colour of their collars is wildly beside the point. Jarman's men and women live outside society on the edge of imminent horror. Most are dying for the day's first fix or drink.

> Outside it hurts to open my eyes. The pink flamingos still have price tags on them. Heat steams in the road, the moss-backed elms dry, ready to crumble or burst into flame. I am running with sweat and toxins.
>
> My father moved to the north side to labour in the huge diesel shop, trains humping all night inside the grass berms, flowering my childhood dreams metal, swearing and coupling. I am parched. My mouth forms phrases. I have the beer.

Not all the stories are equally successful. But Jarman had the talent and the literary wisdom to understand from the beginnings of his career that *words* and their deployment were his answer and salvation. He had the insight and courage to sacrifice grammar and punctuation and tradition to grab immediacy.

Mark Anthony Jarman's career unfolded—exploded—into

New Orleans is Sinking and *19 Knives. Dancing Nightly in the Tavern* is a glittering book, the first expression of a literary samurai.

John Metcalf
Ottawa, ON, June 2006

Cowboys Inc.

Desire itself is movement
Not in itself desirable.
T. S. Eliot

Drunk sheets of light, the ancient Volvo angle-parked in the Interstate rest area. Cooler inside: Jankovitch, slouched at the sink in shorts, a gaudy bowling shirt. A boy and a father yell at each other over the rush of hand dryers. BAM! Hot air whooshing loudly. "You warsh yer hands?" BAM! "Hahn?" yells the kid, two feet from his father. Ironchild cranking up on the government can, searching sideways for the mainline while Jankovitch fiddles impatiently with the button over the sink to get the weather radio. "YOU WARSH YER HANDS I SAID!!" The needle sinks into flesh, the father's new cowboy hat is blown from his small head. "YA!!" screams the kid in reply.

And Ironchild has bought the farm, the last shot too pure or maybe just a piece of talc jamming an artery and boom, lights out, works still jabbed teetering in his pocked arm. "YOU WARSH YER FACE?!" yells the father now, brushing dirty water from his felt hat. Jankovitch sees Ironchild, sees, closes the cubicle door behind him, grunting as he manoeuvres Ironchild's now heavy body, propping his paratrooper boots inside the toilet bowl, the dead man's armpits damp, his skinhead cut bristling at Jankovitch's face, breath gone, skin white, clammy, Jankovitch fumbling, grunting. "YOUR FACE. YOU WARSH YER FACE!" Jankovitch waits sweating: *Leave fuckheads*. The father and son finally exit. Jankovitch grabs the car keys, the German knife, wallet, cash and by reflex, the ziploc of powder; it has sentimental value. Jams the cubicle door shut with a matchbook wedge, scrawls *Out of Order* on a paper towel on the door. That should buy a few hours, hopes Jankovitch, maybe a day or two. With the warrant in Missouri there is little choice.

A State Trooper walks in leaning to the mirror to stare into his own red eyes, takes out a pink comb. "Comb the wind outta my hair," he says into the silence. He peers at the Out of Order sign, at Jankovitch's pen and heads for a further cubicle, undoing his big leather belt and pants. "Damn," he says. "Can put a man on the friggin' moon, what's it take to keep one of these shitters running?" "Yessir," speaks Jankovitch, sidling outside into yet another realm of meat. The sun makes him sneeze. A legless cowboy sells pencils from a wheelchair, duded up for the tourist kingdoms of heat and light. Jankovitch peels a one from the dead man's cash, gives it to the legless cowboy, the sin eater. "Much obliged pardner." Buicks buzz in the sun like bluebottles. Jankovitch sneezes again. A mother: her child wants a drink. "Shut you up or I'll break your face." More sacred bonds, semi-trailers angled everywhere in the glint. "Where you headed?" she says. "West," Jankovitch says. "You have a good day now sir," she says. "I will try to," he says. He walks to the rusting Volvo. Lightning Hopkins is dead now. Murray the K. John Wayne with his Nevada cancers gutting him like a fish. Virginia has her feet up in the front seat perusing *Thin Thighs in 30 Days*. There is so much light around her, a haze of hooks, too private. She looks up at Jankovitch, at the book. "I used to have a fair vocabulary . . . kind of quit 'bout the time I started selling lawnmowers." All Jankovitch can think of is the bald janitor at the party insisting to Ironchild that all dances evolved from the polka, saying it over and over with such seriousness that Ironchild hit him and now Ironchild in the cubicle for some janitor to find. Jankovitch stares up the road into the grasshoppers and hundreds of flattened jackrabbits. Why this worship of death and youth, of carelessness?

THE BIG COUNTRY. Asleep. "Wake up. Wake up." Near Easter time too, the Lenten tornadoes touching down around the women in their gardens. "Wake up buddy." Jankovitch closes his eyes to rise from cancerous dreams of flooded towns dying in silt rivers, farm land leaching out, drifting away, Ironchild toying with his needles and grinding blue pills in the failing light. "Wake up." Jankovitch jerks forward. "What?" Saliva drying upturned in his stupid throat. Crows, nothing grows, gears gnash in testimony to bad driving and the Swedish car's endless capacity for punishment. This is the way they go: "We want you to drive again, okay?" Virginia in fedora and shades leaning over the seat to gently rouse Jankovitch who's down in shitkicker country again ("put the cunt back in country"), swinging hard across the blue plains and raggedy-ass cottonwood, the endless flight through pale aspens and truck stop botulism, K-Mart snakeskin cowboy boots, cheating songs, box elders. This is just after the grain elevator blew over to Missouri: burned for days and they couldn't get at the bodies.

In the blind pigs and roadhouses, lizards cringe under the crashing rain of Wurlitzers and chicken bones. God and country are toasted. "Wake up buddy." Jankovitch supposed to be loyally prone and deceased in the smouldering ruin, not snuck off from work in the cross-tracks bar when the elevator spontaneously disintegrated, providing half-cut Jankovitch an all-too-neat opportunity to duck the warrant, the women and possible pregnancies, the big debts, the whole grieving family. Missouri: Show Me State, population 4,676,000. Capital: Jefferson City. Best diner in Nine Eagles county: Hines Cedar Crest for Sunday brunch, fried chicken and eggs and thirty-one salads or Saturday night fishfry with their special recipe for carp and catfish. Jankovitch stares at the outlines of her breasts shifting in a soft halter top. "Yes yes, I'm awake now."

WITH DARKNESS they are well west of the rivers but still men stand on backwater banks spearing huge fish with three-tined pitchforks. Sand roads snake the steep hills, crossing and recrossing the smaller brackish channels. The café menus slowly lose fresh catfish and perch, buffalo fish. The Volvo zig-zags north, west, past Indian paintbrush and stallions glowing beside them, hooves sparking on bits of gravel, the four cylinder engine an absurd fire sucking air cool through two carbs: night an azure tunnel. Loosening spring begins in mud, ends in mud, calves on the ground or splaying forefeet, endless births and fecundity terrible at times and Jankovitch still young, he thinks, pushing thirty but it seems he's always pushing thirty. He stares at Virginia once more, graceful in angora and her hat, smells her perfume. Willows flank the dust, cold beer and greased wheels carrying west over the big country, west and then north up the clean coast, dark rocks in sand, congealing circles slowing to the still point in the center of the wheel, the union of radii, like a Hollywood wagonwheel; the Volvo's polished baby moon hubcap, a still blurred eye enroute to wherever, Eureka, the north Oregon coastline, maybe Port Angeles and the Blackball ferry splitting the freezing water. Always speeding, Jankovitch deliberately ignoring the warning signs. Ironchild curled mumbling into his own world in the dim backseat, hunkered with his cache and his vomiting paranoia and god knows what in his head and arms; "I need my muscatel so I can be well. . . ." Virginia and Jankovitch drop into the golden bowl of earth. Green evenings, wind blowing the first warmth of the season.

The three of them stop in small towns to purchase fresh crusty rolls, bakery donuts, creamery butter, chicken fried steak and a huge block of Wisconsin cheese. In Rook River locals stare at Ironchild; shivering, a blanket wrapped like a cerement around his shoulders, his skinhead cut, tinted mod glasses, Union Jack T-shirt, zippered army pants and clunky paratrooper boots.

A woman is a support system for a cunt, he says and Virginia slaps him hard. Jankovitch bides his time, comforts Virginia. Trust now in Christ, yells Ironchild at the bar. This ain't no disco! Ironchild, I gave you my purse, says Virginia. Where did you put it? You gave me your purse, har har. Put money in thy purse. He lights a smoke, spreads slow large hands into a laugh. Har har, go dance. Trust now in Christ, go dance with Jankovitch, all this bullshit . . . SWAT squad could come in here . . . they get nothing from me. Hey listen, striking a fist down. This stuff's *good*. All you guys, ever been *busted*?

Busted? Gimme that damn cowboy hat, you ever ridden a horse, huh? Go dance you two, go dance.

Virginia and Jankovitch are silent. Ironchild flicks ash, knocks over a chair, recounts a dispute over another chair, another bar, something about a door, it is hard to tell. So I went outside, he says, I was hammered but calm you know, came back in later and drank and they say I'm barred for life, eighty-sixed. They can't do that can they? Hell . . . can't go to prison for life. His sad puzzled look.

Plastic deer on the lawns and they drive, skies cleaned and deer on the lawns, police flashers bouncing on the grottoes to the Virgin Mary. Jankovitch throws away his wallet. *The Pom-Pom Girls* has played all year at the local drive-in. The mechanical woodpeckers every dawn and in the mist cattle bellowing as if being gored or, as Ironchild allows, involved in some heavy fucking. Looking longingly at two horses by a rusting corncrib, neck to neck in the filtered light, Jankovitch envies their ease with one another (and he pressed the accelerator further to the wood, lighting for the territories cursing himself to *wait till this mythless century shuts down and my fucking hair falls out and what's it matter*, only wanting to be pure again, undiseased, to do it over again but this is not in the cards and then the merry-go-round of blue flashers, the man touching the night's perimeter, the grottoes, to tell of just what can and can't be done on this religious back road, in this century, the limits, the tickets Jankovitch can never hope to cover).

The two awkwardly switch seats so that Virginia, the ex-schoolteacher, the best driver, and not Jankovitch, hands a licence to the police. A spiderweb over her face, the police a floating border astride the traveller's inarticulate hunger for happy trails, miles, women, to pay later. The dead man won't stop drinking or shooting and Virginia cries in the tent. She washes his needles dutifully. The year before nursed him from a yellow bed of hepatitis. Go dance! he yells. In October he locked her in the cold room afraid of losing her, knowing. She washes his needles. Just a little toot! he cries now, crashing into the undergrowth.

GLAUCOUS GULLS, POLYGLOT. A tongue moves among lips. For Your Well-Being: We have provided electric hand dryers to protect you from disease. Stinking hands, cancer will be kind to me.

He took her by the wrists, the white hills where there were no trees because at first she laughed, a joke on Ironchild leaving him but then realizing it is serious; yelling, yanking on the emergency brake until it reeked of smoke and friction. Hitting Jankovitch. Pull over, pull over Jesus, where is Ironchild? And Jankovitch yelling back, look he's dead I can't stay, not with that warrant over my fucking head and me supposed to be dead in Missouri (realizing then he didn't even know who owned the car). If you want to stay (didn't want to know). If you want to stay. And there were no trees (took her by the wrists because . . .). Only boulders that looked to have fallen from another planet into the sculpted twisted badlands, her crying, crying, the paltry rivers, crossing and recrossing the same goddamn rivers all day (me supposed to be dead, not him), all day she wouldn't stop crying, no trees and always seeming to be a third with them. Her light eyes and dark eyebrows, brownish-blond curls, bony cheeks and earrings giving her an older, lupine appearance. Both crying.

They washed and took some of the assortment of pills. She wore makeup now and in the new heat wore only panties and a bra, the white strap bisecting her sleek back. The vehicle, Yellowknife, velar voices sunk in throats, seats.

THE PLAINS FILL WITH WIND. The rattling seed pod logic of cut fields, the plotted grid striped with ditches of purple weeds and prairie flowers: bluebells, black-eyed Susans, hawkweed. Wild sunflowers bend and bend. In the distance, beyond Virginia's freckled profile, rain slopes in indigo columns. "It will be rain tonight." A satellite dish perches over the cinder block motel and rented roughneck trailers. Oil and cattle dividing the empty quarter. "Let it come down." The fine curves of her throat, wisps of loose hair about the schoolteacher's cheek, the back of her neck, her throat. Water hangs silver in mid-air. A razor. In the cinder block rooms around them, the drugstore cowboys lie on narrow bunks as Jankovitch moves into her for the first time, as hard as he can, knows he will come too soon, but doesn't slow, resigned, the cheap bed shrieking, the bored cowhands around them sipping longnecks and gazing at *The Waltons* or fuckflicks from the satellite dish, the strange fruit of the space race; grainy breasts spread in blue windows, huge thighs kicking over the republic's dark fields, eyes always on the screen, uncapping mickeys or lighting Chesterfields by reflex, eyes locked blindly on the oval screens where a tearful John Boy won't shoot the doe or giant vaginas open in a red glistening. They leave their hats on indoors, not a movement is wasted. Jankovitch wears the dead man's hat for a while as he fucks her, his being shrunken and full of peanuts. "Goodnight John Boy," the cowboys murmur in unison or hum along to

The Ballad of Palladin by Johnny Western, the ferret-like cowhands grasping wads of toilet paper, the lone couple coming, this, uh, can't, yes? Go, Jesus, go on. Is it safe? They age in his arms. Always.

"BE BACK SHORTLY." The dead man jolts to a halt in one joyless burg, a county seat with Italian Gothic courthouse on the customary rise, to break into BigValu Pharmacy, the two, three, nervous, hurry hurry Christ hurry, sweat tingling in odd angles down the shirtback cotton, eyes up and down the spooked alley, the big metal doors creaking, Jesus H. Christ will you hurry Ironchild? and he does, smooth, strangely efficient, escaping back into the anarchy of flight and vision splintered between coasts.

No wonder they hate the outsiders, thinks Jankovitch, no wonder the beatings in pool halls, the hair-trigger shooting over twenty cents of spilled popcorn. Where you from? they'll ask. Yazoo, he says giggling. Yazoo City. Fuck what a mouth. Going back soon too, love Yazoo and so on. He looked like a fag golfer in that purple shirt and he wouldn't leave it fuckin' alone. Yazoo! They took him. They're not from here. No one is from here.

Jankovitch wakes on the Interstate tense, nervous, unrested. Dreams of nothing, of close to nothing, of parallel nations of ropes and posses, the borders, the chases, cowboys crossing champaign and treed slopes, chase dreams, crossing ancient sea bottoms now in grain and being forced to face things at the fence, the tree. In nightmares begin responsibilities and Ironchild worries Jankovitch, doing more Talwin when he can, pacing it with the stolen Demerol, cans of Busch, chocolate bars, garbage collecting at his feet. Shadows under his bright eyes.

Ironchild grins, smelling of sweat and borax; he never changes his T-shirt. Virginia and Jankovitch change once or twice a day. In South Dakota, above a reservoir at sunset, they buy beer and a good hairbrush on the dead man's credit card. Jankovitch's scalp itching. Spring flooding, rivers twist into blue-red evening. Ironchild passed out again, breathing noisily. Virginia calmly signs, Jankovitch nervous, not wanting to leave his name. They wash up.

Passing the derelict feedlots at Ash Hollow and then the Cowboy Church of Christ, its sign in looping lariat script, a polished ochre cow horn over the doors. Every time they pass a church Jankovitch shudders at the sharp steeples, sees the works stuck in Ironchild's white fish flesh, teetering on the toilet, another dead country.

After showering at the YMCA: Ironchild in the stairwell, a wrestling mat hung. He pounds it fiercely, his fists blurred. Wouldn't want ten of those to the head would you? he says. Uh no.

Jankovitch is part of the car now, no longer stepping out to stretch or exercise, hands nailed to the wheel, staring ahead, smelling the gasoline fumes, the road everything; moving, random, sweet, his lost colours. Drive and drive until everything flies apart. Then breakfast. Worried, Virginia has to pry him from between the Volvo's rusting fenders. Inside Ironchild turns at the table: "Got me a problem back in Missouri, people say this, people say that 'bout me. But I don't know who. Buddy, give me a name, I wanna be kissed when I get screwed." He takes a drink of lukewarm water, stares sadly over the white plains. Jankovitch buys a local paper: HE HUNTED DOWN 13 YOUNGSTERS WHILE DRIVING SHINY RENTAL CAR. The Red Brigade's Giovanni Ciucci confessed: "I could not succeed in seeing him as an enemy, but only as a man who was sleeping." Finds an article: Jehosaphat Flats—An investigation is underway into a series of drug-related break-ins at medical offices in the northwest area of the state over a two day period this week. . . .

"Y'all want coffee? Y'all want this on one ticket?" Jankovitch jumps, a huge waitress, wrinkles between blue earrings. They ask for tea, pigs in a blanket, *Huevos Rancheros*, chicken fingers, beans, unsweetened grapefruit juice, ambience, greasy ions. Jankovitch stares at a mass of eggs on the hot grill palpitating like a yellow heart. Ironchild eats in seconds; it is there, it is gone. A cockroach or something on Jankovitch's thigh. He flicks it down and stomps. After, he wonders if he was hallucinating and keeps lifting his foot to make sure it is there.

A local saunters in and the waitress pulls him a diet Pepsi before the man has spoken. The cook stands with a greasy spatula: "That be Pepsi and tenderloin or tenderloin and Pepsi?"

"Either way. Got any good numbers left?" He puts money on a football game.

"You wanna give me your tip now," says the cook, winking at the waitress. "I get off early." The cook laughs. "Last tip he gave me: Don't . . . eat . . . yellow . . . snow," drawing out each word slowly for effect. Outside there are apples and blood in the gutter. Jankovitch and Virginia and Ironchild stare. The floating wood of the storefronts. The primary colors surrounding the car, the food on their breath.

NIGHTCRAWLERS NINTEY CENTS. Jankovitch wipes the film of grease from his forehead, eases sweaty shirtback from the seat, reads the ads painted roughly on sagging white trash barns, reads them: Bull Durham, Mountain Dew, Do You Want Freedom *Joy* Heaven? Wrigley's Spearmint—Chew It After Every Meal, nodding he will, of course he will. Ironchild out of it again in the backseat and she looks over with her cat-like eyes, the plains a bed, a white sea behind her head and she bends her long hair into his lap as he drives jolting, surprised, uh yeah, her bending into him and Ironchild stirs, wakes in the back seat: Where we now, buddy? asked sleepily. Near Red Mound, whispers Jankovitch, not knowing or caring where the hell they are. She's sleeping, he says, still whispering, lying. Ironchild rubbing his eyes like a child and Virginia calmly covers Jankovitch's unzipped lap with a jean jacket, feigns sleep. Jankovitch thinks of Ironchild's flailing fists in the green stairwell.

Wanna stop? You thirsty?

Not this cowboy, says the dead man.

Wash up? Maybe coffee to go?

Whatever, whatever, he says, sounding irritated now, staring out.

Gotta get gas. Ya.

Some fun now, thinks Jankovitch. Ironchild begins a groggy wash of talk about the last time he got busted, how two Blackfeet made the mistake of looking at him so he knocked out the closest with a flying kick, pounding the inert form on the sidewalk. The second man fled behind a Pontiac to draw a knife from his boot. He sliced Ironchild's arm and shoulder. (Ironchild stretches his T-shirt, points to the scars, the proud flesh knotted in lines.) Bleeding, Ironchild grabbed the long black hair, smashed the man's face into the hood over and over, face, metal, face mashed flat, bone, caved-in bone, a noise like a garbage can lid. A fat man intervened with a tire iron, complaining of the mess and dents in the hood. Yazoo City. With a reddening shirt Ironchild fled fueled on adrenalin and diet pills until tackled by an off-duty cop in the alley behind the Army & Navy. Two male prostitutes were dragged into the same remand cell arguing, one bragging a john on The Hill had paid him fifty bucks. The second outraged, screaming "Ten! Ten dollars! No more, never." They fought and two older prisoners broke them apart then forced them to "give face" as Ironchild called it. "Better than my wife," growled one. "These guys know what they're doing."

Viriginia rises. "So did you indulge?" she asks, sounding jealous.

"Not this cowboy," Ironchild says. "I told 'em I'd watch for the screws."

Jankovitch has the distinct feeling he should hop out and grab a Greyhound at the next town. Why do I stay? he wonders. This is what he thinks Ironchild has: Talwin, black beauties, NoDoz, an antihistamine that Jankovitch cannot pronounce, the Demerol, grinding teeth, a jumpy walk. Ironchild may have more, they cannot be sure. He slurs some words.

In Wyoming the three of them buy cowboy hats, one of those moments. A beautiful corner of the state, beef country, blue mountains in the distance. Inexplicable nostalgia, cattle and green cool hills shouldering up from each side of a hissing current, the spring prairie torrent deceptive, dangerous. Blue mountains in the distance.

Their three shadows lean and roll as if stranded in an open boat: he drove, she drove, then the other drove, and then she drove and he drove, they drove and they drove, climbing toward the higher passes and mining towns. Under red nimbo-stratus, black hulks staring at the soil, stoic, bovine, stray spears of grain confused in last year's stubble.

Speed, speed, the counties blurring two centuries past the cracked glass, the inevitable descent into fatigue and puzzlement, climbing, her stockings beside his leg and the giddy wonderment of these distances and her new body, the vast plateaus, the new comprehension of geography, the million schizoid nations of North America. His maps: Jankovitch can still see the nuns and old school maps, dusty Mexico, El Chichon pouring crud into the air to the south, sixty million tons of ash; sulphur dioxide gas, salt and dust in a cloud circling the earth every ten days, altering the weather over the crazy checkerboard squares of the Union and pink Canada almost tangible, breathing to the north. Jankovitch reaches a fevered hand out the window toward the sleeping cool light, another into her as she drives, the arbitrary borders, the blue silos of sweetgrass, Texas Playboys and Joy Division in an unlikely combination on the radio. The ash circles the alfalfa and red clover.

Jankovitch drives the peaks in his favourite red T-shirt, found on the ski hill after a knee-wrenching wipeout. The ligaments still sore. Virginia silent, thinking, watching Jankovitch's arm muscles in the bright shirt, leaning with the small car, physically forcing it stiff-armed through the mountain curves and hairpins, accelerating, always accelerating, whooping, swooping downhill until the red needle is buried, in the rearview the dead man floating up white-faced from his attempt at rest on the stiff back seat. Jankovitch laughing at his worried expression.

Hey buddy, you always drive this fast? asks the dead man. I'm getting rocked around a mite.

We're making good time, go crank some more shit.

You got a lot of class you know that do you buddy. Maybe you should try a little of this shit, cool your jets quick, I don't think it's ever been stepped on.

Me? Cut the crap, I got enough problems without yours.

No buddy, I mean it.

The wind smells nice, she says. I feel sick, she says.

You been chippying too? asks the dead man.

Into Silver Valley. Wind off the hardpan plains shakes the saskatoon berries. Raybeats' *Pirhanna Salad* jangling the FM out of some Montana college town.

Have a line.

North, losing spring, all that. Winter wheat, the ancient pulls, secrets draining lives. The threat of rain at night, dependent on women and supermarkets. I'm dead, thinks Jankovitch. Night. Why does she stay? She blames my stupid brooding and outbursts on an Irish temper, ranting after a bad pool shot, a flat tire. Her thin form in the flawed mirrors and motels, bent in the modern dance: the bars neon atolls in the buffalo grass. Her nostrils, her bare heel on a wooden floor tightening her calf and his groin, the way her legs run together against his throat. He wants her in the room where she stands, her brown back to him, ironing blouses in her underwear until he tears the panties from her, nuzzling her ass and climbs her spine to lean, a speck of caution crawling insect-like in the back of his mind but body and cock push on until the ironing board crashes down and they're dazed reptiles crabbling the floor's beer cans as the dead man comes out of the bathroom in torn Fruit of the Looms, haggard and silent behind yellow light, sniffs, moving each side of his mouth. Jankovitch waits for the punishment he has courted, the ten to the head or kicks along the rib cage but Ironchild turns back to whatever, his constipation from Talwin or recalling which arm or leg is next.

Embarrassed, Jankovitch falls into the prickly armchair, sinking into dreams of curtains flashing on her metal skin, Ironchild in the tub, tides of highway traffic behind her shape and her shape, no longer pissed off, wakes him to move to the bed half asleep, dressing quietly and falling into each other's riddled karma, the big curves push-pull-pushing and everyone must know this bliss, cats falling in the air and gone into the rhythms of sleep.

THE DIN OF THE ROADSIDE BAR: horrible coughing through drooping moustaches, the suction sound of fridge doors, words sputtered out, boots slamming the rough wood. Nearly all the men have lost one thumb roping calves, the digit caught and ground away between the coarse rope and the hard leather saddle horn. Money changes hands at the pool tables. Glasses smash. The men hang up yellow slickers, order a shot and chaser and squint and blink on the front stoop into the drunken light to the north, throats cleared of the railroad dust, spittle mixed with dust and hardened Montana mud; the payments waiting, going crazy in their thin grey skin, itching for some odd congress.

Sad bluegrass and cowboys jumping up and down, up and down, yahoo, on some poor clown in the parking lot, their playground. Lookit those sonsabitches, says Ironchild. They know how to live. Yippee Ti Yi Yo! White crosses in the ditch where the highway curves down from Canada.

Jankovitch fills his hat with beernuts and leaves it on the picnic table where they eat from it as they drain can after can of Foster's. Rain falls overnight. In the sere morning the hat is shrunken, bent, unrecognisable, sodden and floating with peanut skins and sugar. Virginia laughs, her kiss a hint of tongue between her lips. She's his only sure thing. Balling the jack across shale and limestones, the faulted anticlines and sawtoothed ridges, into the cirques. Jankovitch contemplates his fucked-up life: buzzing the awful country, drunken prairies and basement rock, evading responsibility and age, ignoring the mirrors, used clothes; *fuck it man*, never any money, never a car, renting rooms, alternately cultivating and blowing liaisons, wandering tired and staying with friends, lovers, bumming off relatives, in motel dives, on bus seats, couches; it gets old. No fatted calves left for this cowboy.

HALLWAY AIR, FLIES GOING CRAZY. She comes out of the shower. Jankovitch watches his cock disappear into her. Do you like to hike? Jesus yes, I like to. O God. You *like* to *hike?* Jankovitch thrusting on each verb. Fuck yes, love hiking, fuck. So. . . . His hand holding the back of her neck, closer and closer to her until he feels he will disappear, his heart beating through her into the mattress.

ROADS SLICK, ANOTHER WHITE CROSS in the Montana ditch, another sign ignored. Rain soaks into the corrals and manure. Downhill to a curve at the bottom of the hill and the car is sliding sideways, just about through the curve and the rear left wheel catches the edge. Is it rolling Bob? Yes, rolling trees and horizon, roll and lay flat and spring up again spinning in the headlights, cans in the air, then stopped and steam from the radiator and tick-ticking from the dead Volvo dribbling out oil. Headlights still on, pointing. Jankovitch grins through splintered teeth because now, helpless, they await the ghouls from the pre-fabs, John Law with his flashing baubles and squeaking holster. Caught in the straps, the straps, his arm at an unnatural angle; now they are hung upside down miles past Little Big Horn and Virginia's face is a strange star, her ruined mouth leaking blood into a spreading stain over his clothes and though it may well mean she's still alive he wishes the dripping would cease because the car is on its roof and he can't stop puking up the last of the Wisconsin cheese. His one sure thing.

Border dreams, cuts himself from the wreck. Turn these fucking headlights off before the ghouls get wind. Finally. Staggers to the slick road and the next high plains cowtown, buys Levi's and a pearl-button shirt, tosses a bloody bundle in the weeds. He can't keep food down. Bruised ribs out like a dog's. He wants a bus to the clean coast, to start over, away from the binges of deceit and drinking, the trail of abortions and car washes, mescal and frozen grins, reckless driving, drinking. New Gleem! Fights The Enemies Of Your Mouth. He swears he's going to change. Starting Monday.

There is too much light at the border; at the stainless steel table they appear ready to dine. These people dress and dream in uniform, dream of the fabled pipelines, donkeys and powder caches. This is their lair, try and tell them it is a false border, that none of it matters. Jankovitch imagines the sick line of questioning: anything to declare? Ha: where can you start. He remembers all the women, the grain elevator turning to atoms, maybe he's still there—but he recalls the great timbers and chunks splintering outside the neon bar. Ashes, water, the stench of grain burning the back of his nostrils. Fuck 'em, he's alive, in flight.

But there at the border with the guards at the ferry terminal is the dead man, in of all things, a fucking suit. Ironchild in a suit! Shaven with a tight white grin and waving a paper. Jankovitch does not have to read it to know his own scrawl: *Out of Order.*

All the women on the bus, there are only women on the bus, turn back to stare at Jankovitch in his sling. He wishes for Virginia now. Now he sees they are all pregnant and staring at him accusingly. A blade in his hands. With his good arm he presses it to his throat. The ziploc. He is washing, washing his hands in the can. Anything to declare? Jesus. He reads the green ticket: I Plead Guilty To The Offense As Charged And Will Pay The Penalty As Proscribed. *Terribilus est locus este.*

Where is Virginia?

Did you eat the last of the cheese? Her soft drawl. Washing. Yes, Virginia I confess, the last of the good Wisconsin cheese. El Chichon's ashes circle one more time. The strap keeps falling from her ivory shoulder. He replaces it but it keeps falling and falling from her ivory shoulder.

That's How Strong My Love Is

"He likes to pound on me," mutters the woman from the next table, staring past Hank into some blurred distance of her own making, into her thick drunk history. And Hank is on the wagon, sipping warm Canada Dry, squinting to follow the hockey game, trying to ignore the reverberating bar crowd, to ignore this irritating woman at the table beside his. He is forced to converse with his friend Mohawk in whispered asides—how to rid themselves of her?

"My son." Her fingers at her neck playing with a crucifix. She turns to face their table. "He put me in emergency twice this year."

The snowy screen blinks from a high corner: Canucks and the Habs tied. Hank's money, two hundred dollars, riding on Vancouver. Ghostly players drift on the ice, shadowed, the sound a murmur, punctuated by whistles, bodychecks bashing the boards.

Receiving no response from Hank, the woman leans the back of her head against the whitewashed wall. Hank looks at Mohawk's straw-yellow hair, lowered over a steaming bowl of house chili. Two sleek young men pass holding hands. Cowboy shirts: long white fringes swinging from the black silk, fancy red embroidery, the smell of poppers on them.

"Jesus," growls Mohawk, glancing at them with a mouthful of hot chili, shaking his head in disgust. "Old Roy Rogers must be rolling in his grave." His green eyes shadowed under a fringe of blond hair.

"Is Roy Rogers dead?" asks the woman, overhearing. "I knew Trigger was; I believe Roy had him stuffed and put in his basement."

The bar groans as Lafleur slips the puck under the pads of Hanlon, the Vancouver goaltender. "Shit," says Hank. "They scored a goal and I missed it."

The woman swivels at her lone table to see what Hank is excited by. She peers up at the screen. "Hockey still? Lordy lordy, it's the first day of spring."

"Yeah yeah, spring."

"Tomorrow is Sunday. When will he settle down?"

"What the hell is she talking about?" whispers Mohawk, shovelling runny chili between his lips with a plastic spoon.

The woman chatters while Hank wonders why she had to sit beside them, why did he come here to stare at women, at his hands, at the dealers in their night watch toques squeezing through the maze of cramped pine tables to get to their imported beer. The scented cigarette smoke, the pocked choruses tugging at sleeves, buying and selling Colombian, junk, Flight 714s, phenobarbital, wading the Maritime atmosphere of ships' paintings, knots and navigating lanterns, the vermilion exit sign a small globe, floating, flashing in the azure haze.

Puzzled, the hovering manager glances at the woman, at Hank, at the woman again. He cracks his knuckles loudly, rubs the soft hands protruding like fish from the stiff cuffs of his suit.

"Is the Bitterroot Hotel still in Juan de Fuca?" The woman leaning to question Hank.

"I don't know. Never heard of it." The insect buzzing of the electric clock. Without asking, the woman lifts one of Mohawk's cold draught and dips at the froth, a chalice brimming with gold. Hank gazes thirstily, notes the throat swallowing, the lipstick left on glass.

"I think she's been cut off," he hisses to Mohawk.

"The Bitterroot was a big place, believe you me."

Raising eyebrows, Hank and Mohawk exchange looks. Mohawk pulling on a Player's, the smouldering cigarette an extension of his lip, its smoke laying a white scar on his face.

"Seven hundred people," the woman insists, stabbing a wrinkled finger and heaving forward in her creaking seat.

Mohawk tears at a hunk of French bread with his teeth, pissed off because she's drinking his beer, stares at Hank. Hank shrugs: what can I do? The bass line buzzes, drags thudding. Big Kahoona, the bar manager, paces nervously behind the old-fashioned draught taps. Hank is reminded of a losing hockey coach prowling the bench.

"Hank. Are you hungover today?"

"Is the pope Polish?"

"Not too hot a party."

"Never any women, someone drinks my booze. Why do we bother?"

"They tell me he's no good!" interjects the woman from

her table. "That I should give up on him!" She quietens. "He's a good boy. Came home and his house empty, their dream home, Spanish furniture and all she took. He's out working. Two thousand dollars that hussy ran up on the Chargex. . . ."

"Hmm."

The woman slouches low in her chair as if exhausted, a dark lambswool coat draped low on her shoulders in an attempt at seductiveness. Makeup colours her skin thickly; harsh eyebrows pencilled above cheeks rouged, perfumed. Her pink pants depress Hank. And on her feet, slippers, silver slippers; dressed to go out on the town. She loosens her wrap to bare the shoulders of her white blouse.

"My, my. It's warm in here don't you find it?" the woman fluttering a hand past her lavender cheeks and rough dabs of lipstick. The world wheeling, the weight of the turreted hotel piled above her, the stone railroad hotel draped with ivy and sinking into the mud flats it was built on the century before.

A fisherman in a green mackinaw lumbers past, selling fresh shrimp to the patrons.

"Seventy-five cents a pound," notes Mohawk, tucking motel matches inside his black vest. Not a bad price," he says through his cigarette. The woman leans to them.

"My name is Mary. I've been drinking all day," she states flatly, pouring salt, then pepper into her beer, the pepper lying like iron filings on the white foam. "I can't get drunk."

"Have you had anything to eat, Mary?" asks Hank.

Pauses between her sentences, her head lowered, gathering strength, lifting her curled skull, with some effort, to speak.

"Nome, not today." She adds tomato juice now. "My boy was supposed to come over for dinner. I had it all fixed nice but he never showed. Pork chops," she confides with a sly wink. "You like pork chops? Smothered in my special gravy, with mushrooms and peas and stuff." She leans further. "Yes. Why don't you boys come over for a good dinner. You could meet my young niece. A real looker!"

Hank expects another wink. Mohawk plays with his lower lip, dragging it down with his forefinger, baring crooked teeth.

"Pork chops."

The clamour in the bar builds, stuttering codas of reggae, drunks in shadowed corners mumbling broken English. Smoke muzzles the sepia lights that mushroom from the lime-white ceiling. A pretty slinger leans into the orange glow of the cash register, ringing up drink after drink. Mary's fingerbones curl around spun glass. Two hundred fucking dollars, thinks Hank. What got into me? Mohawk stacks neat piles of silver. The slinger smacks more glasses on dark wood, remaining bent over long enough for her cleavage to be perused. Mohawk shifts one pile of coins to her, conceding her tip.

"I woke up real early, looked at three grey walls and got the hell out." Mohawk speaks staring at the table top. "Mild anxiety attack, nothing serious."

"Catholic guilt," says Hank.

"You boys ever read the *Book of Revelations*?" interrupts Mary.

"Listen Mary, I didn't come here tonight to get preached at," snaps Hank. "I can get that at home anytime."

"Who's preaching?" asks Mary, offended. "I had to work to get through it, but everything's in it. Everything. Read it."

"Fuck that noise man." Gingerale coating his teeth, Hank staring morosely at their cold beer, wanting one.

"I believe, I believe in man's intellect. I think we're progressing, improving, to a time, you know, when there'll be no war, no famine, nothing. . . ."

"You must be joking," says Hank.

"Piss on it," pipes in Mohawk, swiping wildly at the hair in his green eyes. Mohawk named, in a moment of drunken inspiration, by his Ukrainian father, in honour of the gas station adjacent to the slaughterhouse and rendering plant that provided his father's first job in the new country.

"I mean, just look at all the shit coming down the pike right now. Everyone rubbing their hands for another war. . . ." His father's darkened eyes and hawkish nose, his mother's blond hair over the swarthy East European features. "Hey, there's Noreen." Waving a hand, he leaves Hank to join another table.

"He is a doubting Thomas," says Mary quietly after Mohawk leaves. "Why don't you call me 'Mom.'" Her cigarette, her stare and lashes. "Are you going to come, for dinner?" She brushes the skin of Hank's arm with her fingers. "What's this bandage from?" Hank stares at the bare arm as if it is detached, someone else's limb.

"Gave blood today," he replies, remembering the needle. Slowly, slowly, Mary leans over until her hair rests against Hank's skin. The tan tops of her breasts are visible as the crucifix swings from her open blouse. Tense, he doesn't move his arm. Two young women steal quick puzzled glances at them. Hank imagines the adolescent women seated at lit mirrors before going out; topless, in tight designer jeans, brushing their long chestnut hair, brushing rouge lingeringly to each other's dime-sized nipples and then sliding only sheer silk over their fresh expectant skin, dressed to go out on the town and Mary beside him in her old-fashioned wire bra, directing words woodenly into his tricep. "I'm lonely," she says. "I need a man."

Fuckaround man, Hank thinking, flies crawling the face of the clock, its black hands flanked by life preservers from the HMCS Cowichan, the HMCS Saguenay. The speakers' gargled buzz. Hank laughs inappropriately, giddy, droll. Mary breaks the uncomfortable pause.

"I read Jesse Owens is dying of cancer. The lungs don't you know." Thick dark beams fix the ceiling and walls in a grid, wood dark as lungs. "I can't get drunk. What is that song by Merle Haggard?" She stands, her head framed by a panel of stained glass hung in a wrought iron light fixture. "Where are the washrooms in this establishment?"

Mohawk saunters back. "We have to dump her. You know that."

Hank studies the hard veins snaking the back of his hands. "She wants me to call her 'Mom.' "

"Great. Noreen's invited us to a party on Telegraph Bay Road, out past Smuggler's Cove. Should be more young tail than you can shake a stick at. I hope there's no trouble with what's-her-name." He glances in the direction of the washrooms, then at the young women in silk. Smiles. "So tell me Hank, what is shaking with said hockey game?" Talking to Hank but gazing at the two young women, admiring the curving undersides of their breasts visible in the light through silk.

"Habs are going to take it. I know."

"Your hard-earned money."

"I had to stop watching after Lafleur got the goal. Vancouver made a bad move trading Lever."

"He's getting on."

"Yeah, yeah. Trade for youth."

A sailor leans over from his table. "That damn goalie must be pregnant." His cropped hair and buck-toothed grin.

"Why is that?" asks Hank. A saxophone loud. Trade for youth.

"Because he missed his last period! Haw!"

"Horseshit." Hank rankled by this slight: Hanlon, the goalie, is a personal favourite of his. "He's the fucking franchise."

"Ha. He couldn't stop a beachball from center ice. Helen Keller would make a better goalie."

"Stick it where the light don't shine."

"Screw you too bud."

"Fuck you pongo!" Hank jumping from his chair and Mohawk pulling him back with a strength that surprises them both.

Mary returns as if a referee. "Now boys," she says. "Settle down boys."

"Hank and I are going to a party," says Mohawk, too quickly.

"Oh good," she beams, clutching her sparkling purse. Hank stands to leave, glad to leave. The buck-toothed sailor gives him a sideways dirty look.

"Jesus, Hank. Give me a hand will you," whispers Mohawk.

Hank leans over, hands flat on the gluey table, feeling adrenalin from the argument. "Mary. Mohawk and I want to go to this party *alone*. Okay?" Trade for youth, he thinks. "Nice meeting you Mary."

Mary glares. "Well, well that's just fine. I didn't want to go to your darn party anyways." Dark eyes peering like bits of glass in her pinched face, her orange lips pressed to each other.

Mohawk fiddles with a rat-tail comb that is suddenly in his hand. "Listen Mary. Everyone will be younger than you. And I know I don't enjoy it when. . . ."

"Oh sure, I'll enjoy it. I love young people." She stands up happily to leave with them. "I can't go home." She leads the way out, Mohawk trudging resignedly behind.

"Motherfucker," winces Hank to himself, scooping some change from the table. The young waitress touches his arm. Her hair is dyed platinum blond, a black scarf knotted tightly around her neck like a collar. Her thin neck and shoulders pale as bone china.

"The manager would like to buy you and your friend a round next time you're in."

"All right."

"You know, for taking her off our hands," she says to him. The manager rubs his belly behind the bar. Off our hands.

Hank hurries down the catwalk, plywood creaking under his feet, stepping past the vines and trees at night, the chained rows of ten-speeds. Hank feels his own belly pushing his belt, a piling of unwanted flesh. Nights he lies in darkness, unable to sleep, caressing his belly, rubbing his stomach with puzzlement, like a woman with an unwanted pregnancy: is this really mine? He remembers as a child, driving with his father in the Buick Electra, his thrifty father's pride, the car that Hank would later inevitably smash. Driving to Devil's Lake and the engine overheating on the Church Road, the idiot light blinking red as they travel south through the pale fields of rock left to these farmers by a glacial whim, his silent father, worried, pulling the shining car under the Timber Trail Ranch sign to have the oil checked but unable to open the hood because of a recent hernia operation, explaining to the couple running the ranch that he has had surgery "on his tummy."

Hank rushed to open the hood, deeply embarrassed in front of the couple. They had little sympathy for city people who could afford a cabin on the lake, used genteel words like *tummy* and could not fix their own cars. The couple made a difficult living selling mix, cigarettes and candy, renting sway-backed mares to the summer people, selling gas and breeding child after fearless child to play with the dust-grey chickens and snarling Alsatians. Later the ranch was abandoned, bankrupt. Gone with Hank's early summers were the jars of rock-hard candy in the confines of the aromatic store, the tobacco tins, the stale Oh Henrys and niggerbabies, the white swings at dusk, the seven-cent colas in the pop machines filled with tepid swamp water.

Hank remembers the dark odours of the lake road at night and his thin shape tiptoeing carefully on the sharp gravel to the girl in the damp bathing suit that left her skin pink when he peeled it from her hips for the first time, flies above like fruit, like raisins glued to the sticky strips of flypaper, twisting, twisting behind the drawn curtains. He was thin then. She touched his stomach first. Pull the warped wood shut, the bandage on the screening, her close, thin, close.

"Mary," he asks.

Woodsmoke spices the night, the brisk air more like autumn than spring, a scent of burning leaves mixing with car exhaust.

"Is there somewhere we can drop you?"

Pale kids, on silent roller skates, drift downhill to the harbour, hands loose at their sides except for one last boy hugging a precious case of Kootenay Pale Ale.

"Your car?"

"It's parked at the Glimpse Reef Inn," she answers. "But I don't want to go there. And I can't go home."

"Why? Why not?" Crickets snap in the hotel's rock garden, crows clicking from the groves of Garry oak and red alder.

"I lost my keys and it is too late to wake up the landlady." Peacocks scream from their enclosures on Beacon Hill. "They're all old geriatrics. Old like me," she adds, waiting to be contradicted.

"I've caused enough trouble there already. Merciful God, look at these two," waving her arm as if to conjure the two men, unshaven and both in grubby overcoats, two stiff overcoats shuffling toward each other at the Cormorant Street crosswalk.

"Hey buddy, what's on at the soup kitchen today?" asks one without slowing, his eyes thick in a face the dark texture of burnt skin in a frying pan. His hands jump in his pockets.

"Macaroni again," sneers the second, shorter man, a squinting visage beneath a blaze-orange hunting cap. Neither man stops moving as they converse.

"Aw jaysus kee-rist," complains the tall darker man, steering the croaking syllables over his shoulder. Both men speak as if ventriloquists, lips pursed shut, an Adam's apple knuckling each folded throat.

Breathing in the raw night, Hank dances silently away, impulsively leaping trash cans and benches; springy, energetic in his $1.49 sneakers, preserving his youth, starving off the advent of overcoats in $1.49 Day sneakers.

Stopping up the block, he turns, looks back to see Mohawk, ear bent in earnest conversation with Mary, as if one is confessing, the other dispensing benediction, penance. Both push huge bent shadows into the line where the brick of the dust-fed wall meets the shining cobblestone. Crooked, bone-scrolled buildings, remnants of the turn of the century shipping boom, loom over the narrow roadway to hem in the two small figures. The bright shop windows bathe the brick and black-top in glassy surrealistic light. Her woman's walk, swaying up the incline from the chill harbour, the bobbing pink splash of her pants rippling in the sea breeze, the faint click-clack of her slippers stepping gingerly to avoid the worms dried on the walk in brittle S shapes.

"It's a different age."

"Times are hard."

"Yup."

"How far do we have to go?" asks Mary, clutching her coat over her breasts, eyebrows arched, the thin tip of her nose red.

"To the Churchill." Merchants change money behind them under the golden arches, the yellow letter M curving huge as a temple against the indigo sky, DEATH TO THE SICK-OIDS spray-painted by local punk rockers on a giant plastic hamburger.

"I'm cold."

"You're cold."

"I would not have come if I had known it was this far," she grumbles, bent over her silver slippers in an uncomfortable shuffle.

"No one forced you."

She glares up from her toil, her dark eyes and high cheek-bones, her nostrils, her eyeshadow the same blue of the streetlights.

In Bastion Square two men blow on sax and trombone, the

dreamlike brass of their instruments shining dully, knotted fingers honking muted ragtime into the lamps' mists. The sheen of hair slick. Outside the Maritime Museum: a small clan of young women, bikers, junkies, intense winos around the massive anchor. A black police van slows.

"The heat." Staring. "Five-oh."

"Cheese it, the cops!" jokes one and they all laugh. The two young policemen stare at the dull boulevard, at the women. Someone pulls hungrily on a cigarette, sending up a lone spark.

STALE SMOKE BILLOWS UP the stairwell, needles and shoes littering the carpeted steps. A serene young man is led by the bouncers past Mary. His beard is jewelled with blood, the calm skin of his face ripped, crimson pearls easing from the cuts. He stares ahead. The bouncer leans forward, yelling into the bloodied face: "Now get out of here shithead!" Shithead gets out of there, a knee rammed in his crotch like a mongrel's exploring snout, Shithead reeling sideways to the street, eyes rolling slightly as if with pleasure and lips mimicking a tropical fish, "Christ," gasping for the shitheads' Christ. The bouncer stops Mary.

"I don't know that you want to go down there," he says kindly. "It's pretty rough tonight sweetie," as if describing the local riptides or small craft warnings. Rigid, her slippered feet aching, she stares past his bulk, as if still entranced by the brass street music, fixes her stare on the bloody wedding ring near the man's knuckles, and thinking of her own son's broken hands, follows the boys down into the bar's mustard murk.

The room undulates as if underwater. Drowsy heads sway

over tiny tables, potato chips crumbling in laps. A narc waves, lifts a calcareous palm, lazily blessing the yellow walls of his floating kingdom, his punch-drunk battalions knee-deep in fog.

Mary watches a somnolent bartender fill glasses of honey-coloured draught, his practised smirk twisted around the end of a long-ashed cigarette, nimble fingers drumming the bar between orders. He runs a blanched hand through the counter's salty moisture. His neck bulging over the collar, the skinny black tie, the winter-white shirt and beer-fed pot hanging heavily on his thick belt, breasts drooping. Like an old woman's, thinks Mary. Lordy, lordy, where are the boys? The airless chamber shifts in the corner of her eye. A blizzard of cigarette butts on the russet rug. Her eyes water in the smoke, turning the butts into blurry butterflies. She rubs her eyes. The butterflies linger, then metamorphose once more to cigarette ends.

A man with a whitewall haircut snores crookedly in his seat, cropped head tilted, reminding Mary of coming home from the Whirlomat to find her Albert in the chilly kitchen, his wire brush hair black with rain, lunch bucket on the tea-stained Formica, his face white, too white, mouth open, purple work-shirt gaping on his pale and hairless chest, his name stitched in red above the shirt pocket, and Mary moving quietly around her husband's body, adjusting the greasy blinds, preparing the ham and eggs he liked in the evening, thinking everything will be all right, everything will be all right, nails dirty in his still lap, the hands on her each night and rough on her breasts, a man, her breasts, the same wool and sweat smell ground into all his frayed clothes, work clothes, sheets, her, and the same smell released in her kitchen by the rain on the shirt and hair released in this tavern now.

Hank talks with the other behind a pocked plaster column. The far side of the bar. Wending her way toward them, the other gesticulating now, she is unable to hear what they argue of and she thinks of Albert, Jesse Owens, Roy Rogers, others, dead or dying. She passes two tough-looking brunettes shooting pool. One leans over the corner pocket, her nose nearly touching the poised cue, the lit green felt, her freckled breasts swinging loose in an egg-yellow tank top. "Ya, ya fucker, Okay," a scuffle breaking out in the stairwell.

"For Christ's sake Hank. Let's go! We'll split out the back way and I'll meet you at The Kings to buy beer. Okay? Okay?"

For a moment the sleepy patrons are galvanized, as the fists in the stairwell connect dreamily with bone and the bouncers jump in.

Hank studies his hands again, pokes their flesh. "We can't leave her in this zoo half cut."

"She's seen us." Mohawk pulls a crinkled Player's from his hip pocket, touches the speckled paper to his large lips. "A lift to her car and that's it."

Sam Cooke's voice rasps beautifully from the Wurlitzer, a couple waltzing, necking in the wash of steel light, his hand stroking her in rhythm with the machine, waltzing Saturday night in the rotting grain smell of draught and sudsy dregs.

"This is crazy."

"Hank. Find out who won the game. Money's riding, long green."

Mary rejoins them. "Hello. Hello."

"Your car parked by the water?" Hank asking Mohawk.

"Ya. By the water. Ya."

THE WHITE RAILING CHAINS droop over the oil-purple lagoon. Japanese flags slap from the fishing boats along the pilings, ghostly beneath the tarmac esplanade. Channel markers blink into an offshore breeze, the wind in the darkness, silver fir bent tight in the salt. Mohawk steers his canary-yellow Caddy along the seawall, past the greening statue of Captain Cook, past the stone hotel listing into the mud flats. The car's fins and fenders flash under the street lamps, patches of blue rust blooming like sores on the infinite fenders, the yellow fins silent, headlights catching the cedar fronds.

"Just take me, to my car. I'll sleep in my car." Stars above the Chinese graveyard, the flats. The three of them cramped in the front seat, her lipstick an orange glow floating between them.

"Isn't there somewhere you can go to? No one you know?"

"My sister-in-law lives not two blocks from here but do you think I can show my face there?"

The radio snickers to life: *and the forecast is for night and morning fog . . .*

"Well can you?"

a risk of frost . . .

"Get some music on that damn radio."

in low-lying areas. . . . The trinity of faces creased in the poor light.

"I don't care to discuss my family."

". . . sooth the savage beast."

"Turn! Turn to the right!" exclaims Mary at the Thunder Road corner.

"This is not the way to the Reef," protests Hank. The huge vehicle squeals past Tex's Grill, a high animal howl from the old tires and suspension, the passengers thrown close against each other, the intimate smells of powder and Mary's perfumed coat, her neck white, close.

"FBI tires," jokes Mohawk.

"Fucking big Indian?"

"No Jesus, the TV show. You know, tires screeching, screech!"

Mary points the way to a Victorian rooming house in Foul Bay, painted decades ago an ugly shade of magenta, with rough red shingles and a drunken veranda cornering one side, its roof and eavestroughs lumped with dark moss. Fecund beach pine and bamboo cane weave a wall around a corroded Studebaker dead in the red mud drive. An upstairs light gleams the yellow of a cat's eye. Darkness drapes the lower floors.

"This is where the son is?" asks Hank.

Mary shakes as if palsied.

"This where you want to go, Mary?" She nods yes.

"What a dump."

"The son, is this where the son lives?" The one that beats you up, thinks Hank. She nods once more, climbs awkwardly from the depths of the ark-like car. On the buckled walk she cries. Hank guides her nervously over the rutted grass, her soft hand warm on Hank's arm, red mud sticking to her silver slippers. A dog, burying an object near the house, skulks away upon their approach. Like curls of sodden tobacco, moss clings to the crooked porch, the steps' hard edges of cedar shuffled away, polished grey. The main door, thick and scarred, pushes open, unlatched, and Mary moves ahead, her woman's walk, trodding briskly to room number one. She raps quickly.

His hands curled into fists, Hank shifts from foot to foot, his hands fists, clenched in his jeans. How big is the son? he wonders. From the upper chambers drifts down a sound like a cow singing. No answer from behind the battered oak door. For a moment Hank envisions a corpse in a bed.

"Take me to the party with you." Her blouse. "I can't go home. I told you that." She is undoing her blouse, fingers tangling in the slight chain of the crucifix, Hank staring in surprise, his fists still clenched in his pockets, expecting a surly son and not this, her white blouse parting slowly to plump breasts the brown of farm eggs, laid in lace. Hank stares with no idea of how long, the pink pants open now, stares, moves, the singing above loud, the sick momentum, her soft hands on him, the powder, moves, descends, the paint flaking from oak, her lax skin pinned to door number one, her son's door rattling in the warped frame, he moves, hands, stomachs, a long way from the lake and young girl in a damp bathing suit, moves in her, baptized, immersed in age. "Ouch," she says, standing like a statue as he moves, her orange lipstick under him saying "ouch," rises on his toes, someone singing, someone shooting salt and light, swimming in salt and light. He grunts and upstairs the singing ceases. He leans into the wall for a minute, understanding he is ancient, spent. Everyone will be younger than you, he thinks.

Rebuttoned and shaking, Mary moves woodenly into the evening, the virgin season. Pushing across the sky are pale night clouds.

"Any luck?" asks Mohawk. Invisible, he slouches low in the expanse of the pine-scented interior, the fat Cadillac engine turning inaudibly, a pulse felt more than heard. “He’s not here? Hey, don’t all answer at once.”

“He’s not here.”

“I’ll just sleep in my car. It’s the first day of spring,” speaks Mary wearily, her blue hands glowing in the shadows like salt.

“Glimpse Reef is the end of the line,” says Mohawk, revving the big engine.

Papers and garbage slide the streets. Japanese cherry branches swim in the wind.

Mohawk halts the car in the hotel’s bleak lot, and Hank, unable to speak, steps out into sharpening air, the city dead, silence inside the car.

“I’ll just sleep in my car,” she repeats.

“I’m sorry,” says Mohawk tersely. “We can’t fuck around like this all night.” His swearing at her changes things. In the turquoise light of the dashboard, pointed stalks of his blond hair glow eerily over his green eyes.

“Jeez, I don’t need your stupid party, you think I need—at least give me a beer. I’ll pay. Give me a drink.” Fumbling with her iridescent purse.

Hank looks unwell. Mohawk looks at her and Hank, steps slowly to the trunk with the keys, gropes into the dark opening between the pointed fins, moves about finally delivering a bottle for her, holding it up high like a doctor with a newborn baby. He uncaps it with his Swiss knife, foam flecking his knuckles. Wipes them on his pant leg, gives the bottle to the woman. She grasps it, shuffles away.

Hank watches her figure shrinking into a maze of wires and poles, her one hand clutching the beer, the other running soft fingers through her curly hair. Her pink pants and fur-trimmed coat under the lamps' yellow-blue coronas, the silhouette of dark chimneys, thorn-wild hedgerows, the black locusts' iron-dark trunks. Her slight body hesitates, staring as if hearing again the ragtime of her street music. She moves uncertainly to a rusting station wagon, tries the door and slides in the driver's side.

"Take care now Mary," says Mohawk, walking around a car to urinate on low chokecherry and buckthorn. "Christ, methinks I got the diabetes." Fruit trees slant stiffly behind him, new pink blossoms looking out of place on the stark branches.

"You think that's her car?"

"Here's her niece's phone number," says Mohawk, crushing the paper in his hand.

They crumple back into their seats.

"I feel like I just dumped my own mother in a bar parking lot," says Hank. "How is she going to sleep in a car? It's not exactly balmy." He stares blankly at an election poster, cursing, the night tasting like gravel in his throat. "My mother doesn't drink though," craning his head to look at the corroded car, the small brown figure sipping from the glass neck, fingering hair at her temple. Hank breathes in sharply, whistling frigid air over an exposed nerve in a molar, the slight pain welcome.

"Well what are we supposed to do?" asks Mohawk. He leans, turns up the radio to catch the hockey scores, the front seat now roomier, wide. "That lady's crazy," he decides.

"No one at the house," says Hank. "Anywhere."

"We got her off our hands now. Listen, listen Hank. You lucky motherfucker, Vancouver actually beat Montreal! Now you can chip in with gas money to run this tub." He talks on.

Hank reaches into his jeans and counts the silver, moving

the coins across his palm. Money's riding. He wonders about the couple from the bankrupt ranch, where are they at this moment?

Mohawk glances at Hank. Hank stares ahead through the windshield's skin of condensation, light and shadows playing about his face.

"Whatcha staring at?" asks Mohawk. "See something you own, ha."

The car rumbles past the reefs, then the basalt harbour, shale slanting stripes into grey waves breaking below the pink houses sewn to the rock hill, the sky sealed and the cold sea air hugging the small streets with its dark odour. Fog, thinks Hank. He begins to laugh at this. Beyond the breakwater he sees the bank of slate fog, creeping into the harbour mouth, drawn toward land, muffling the ringing of the buoy bells, moving toward them over the herring gulls riding out the night's swells. The radio states the time. Mohawk talks on nervously into Hank's laughter.

Wintering Partners

The young woman stands near the telephone kiosk Trask stood near ten years earlier. You pretend to place a call should the police appear. Her cheeks are reddened by the cold, as if slapped, breath flowering from lips as she shifts foot to foot keeping warm, tapping for a bottle.

"Would you go into the liquor store for me?" Brushes chestnut hair from her face. "A couple bottles of wine? Please?"

Trask decides he owes this much, for the nights when he tapped to get a bottle, when he made the same requests not knowing the prices inside, when the age was twenty-one and men disappeared with your money.

"What kind of wine can I get you?"

He locates her rosé and purchases a mickey of Southern Comfort for himself. When he pushes open the glass exit, she is leaning on the rough brick, her hands deep in the pockets of her blue jacket. Seeing Trask, she stands straight.

Snow moves down the black ice, like chaff. Wind gropes into corners and doorways, seeking exposed skin, cells of heat. Trask hands her the package, her change.

He presses the coins in her palm, small and white with her glove taken off, but she pushes the money into his pant pocket and on tiptoe gives him a quick kiss. His lips are cracked and chapped. A faint scent of Dentyne rises from her mouth. She looks so healthy, he thinks. How old is she?

"I'm going to the dance at St Andrew's," she says, "you know the old hall. . . ." Behind them, drunken oil rig workers pull up in taxis.

"Is that right?" He looks to see if the trolley is near.

"Do you dance?" Swaying, she hugs the wine to her breast as though it is a child.

"Not very well," he says. In high school his dancing was compared to someone walking in a stiff breeze.

"You should come. The old church hall."

Trask steps away carefully on the ice, as if on egg shells, toward the bar. The cold clears his mind: everything is reduced to simple terms. She calls thanks, waves brightly.

Like iron-coloured gargoyles, natives huddle at the stop beneath the black cliffs, smelling of woodsmoke, held together by overcoats and rags, bottles like bits of sky inside a garment. The wind drives shards of ice and snow before them, whips coarse shreds of cloud before the moon, slackens for a moment. Above the empty doorways and frozen clotheslines, white smoke steams from chimneys, lifts into black sky. The trolley comes.

Carson is in The Egypt. Trask was afraid of that. She sits close to a burly rugby player, raising a menthol cigarette to her even teeth, or swinging her hair. The rugby player's moustache droops over his large lips like strands of seaweed. He tilts an Export straight back, bubbles gaping and bursting in the glass.

He clunks the emptied bottle down hard, a hand kneading his stomach, his gaze moving to all corners of the room before returning to Carson beside him. He squeezes her elbow and opens his mouth. She laughs, exhaling air lightly, her blond head nodding as if on a spring.

Carson, from Vancouver, is a psych major, a dorm don, plays intramural volleyball, works part-time in the faculty club and maintains honour grades. She has been married once, and with her tweed and wide-hipped matronly look, appears older than she is. "I just don't have time to get depressed, there's so much to do!" she would tell Trask and he would get depressed listening to her.

"You. You know you're barred." Sid, an aging bouncer, jabs Trask hard in the solar plexus. "So get out of here. *Now*."

From any distance, Sid's nose resembles a purplish light-bulb, but up this close it is possible to see an intricate wiring of black and red veins.

"I'm not staying," shrugs Trask.

"That's right troublemaker," baring his teeth like an elderly spaniel. "You're not staying," and he shoves Trask's shoulder. "We don't need no more trouble here with police."

The map of burst capillaries is the only colour in his face. The last time Trask saw the bouncer's wired nose, two young constables were dragging him from it. One seemed to want to break Trask's right arm so he pushed him. Down at the police station they stopped the elevator between floors, took turns.

"And stay out." Sid shoves him again. Trask trips on a mat, stumbles outside in a cloud, reels backwards into a mound of snow, glimpsing Carson staring through the vapours of the doorway. Her face jerks with recognition and the door slams closed. Trask sits on the gritty snowbank, tossing bits of ice at a shovel.

"Sid, I must admit I don't understand the bouncer mentality," he mumbles to himself. Carson does not come out. The mickey of Southern Comfort is still intact. No one comes out. He stands and dusts off his pants, though there is no dust.

HE CAN HEAR MUSIC outside the church hall. A fat man grabs tickets at the second set of doors, returns a green shred wet with his sweat.

The bands run through some fast Texas Swing, the hall interior smothered in orange light. The band's name is lettered on the bass drum: WIZARD LAKE RHYTHM PALS. Powder is sprinkled on the varnished floor. Couples grapple, trudge across the dance floor. Obese arms pull flabby elbows through the paces, cup shoulders and sweaty backs. Beehive hairdos, plastered and sprayed in place, bow opposite jellyrolls and ducktails. Beer bellies sway and shrink, push into pointed bras and lines of tight panties rolling flesh over elastic.

Trask's eyes become accustomed to the orange light and pulsing crowd. A woman glances over, smiles. She wears a sleeveless top and one arm shows a huge inoculation mark.

The woman from the liquor store is talking with another young woman on wooden benches lining the west wall. They peer around the room as they converse and she sees Trask.

"You made it. We just got here too." She takes his arm. "Come and meet my friend." They are slightly drunk. She smiles at him. "We drank the wine in Coronation Park."

"You must've froze."

"We had to make it fast." She laughs, whispers her name:

Twila. Twila and her friend Sherri wear white blouses embroidered with tiny flowers and lace. They are young and slim compared to the other women. Trask is caught between age groups, belongs to neither. Cowboys fall drunk to the floor.

"The crowd is older than I thought they'd be."

"It's strange," agrees Twila. "We may have the dates mixed up." It turns out the friend who told them does a lot of pharmaceuticals.

"Well, we paid, might as well see what happens." Twila and Sherri find a table while Trask buys tickets for drinks. They lean around a long table littered with overflowing ashtrays and emptied bottles. Trask feels as if he has crashed a wedding reception. The band is catatonic going through *Orange Blossom Special* for the thousandth time but the crowd loves the fiddle tune. Tonight Johnny Asphalt is sitting in with the band on pedal steel. They wing through *Fat Boy Rag*, *Route 66*, a haunting *Ghost Riders In The Sky*—as close to chicken-skin music as this band will ever be. Bits of Kleenex are clotted to Johnny's fresh-shaven chin. A tic works his face as he picks a tricky steel solo. Someone in a Maui T-shirt leans over the table. Sherri leaves to dance with him. Twila and Trask drink quietly as the dark-corner couples hug and gobble at each other's necks.

Mr. Asphalt's steel guitar begins a slow version of *Hickory Wind* and Trask asks Twila to dance, confident of handling a waltz. She hugs herself closely to him, all of her light body, from her head to her ankles, somehow softly pressing against him. Slowly, slowly, they move together and he slides his hand up the silk of her back: she is not wearing a bra. He feels he is dancing with his little sister.

A couple drifts behind in matching blue team jackets, the names *Cliff* and *Shirley* on the respective sleeves. A teased hairdo snagged on the woman's head like an errant magpie nest. Heels knife the floor as Shirley and Cliff click past. Twila leans her head on Trask, a pleasant scent in her hair, like balsam. They dance a couple more.

"Where is Sherri?"

"I imagine the coatroom."

"With that guy?" he asks, feeling protective.

"Every church dance she rummages through the coat pockets."

Trask lifts his head a bit, confused. "What does she get?"

"A couple dollars, bus tickets, lipstick." As they talk, Twila doesn't look up. She moves slowly with him, her head on his chest, fragrant hair brushing the skin of his face.

"Seems risky for the sake of bus tickets."

"I think that's why she does it." She sways without looking up, her hair and the warmth of her length against him, holding him.

THEN AS YOU WALTZ you think how cool Carson was last time you talked, a Friday night and she phones two hours late and then she talks and talks as if all is normal, finally saying, well she has to run, with that forced cheerfulness of hers. Have to run? you ask, wondering what the hell is she up to, this is Friday night, you should be together, but she says she just has to drive a good good friend to work, the poor dear, and then she's going straight home to bone up for a psych quiz. And she has a headache from work. A headache! you think, Jesus. She promised her mother she'd bake some stuff as well and you say nothing now, knowing this is a brush-off but not believing it, she's dumping you. You still there? she asks. Yeah, you mumble. Well, she says lightly, I'll talk to you later.

THE BAND FINISHES WITH *Will The Circle Be Unbroken*. The ticket taker, a Trilby hat on his skull, flicks on fluorescent lights and Trask blinks fiercely, holds his hands over his eyes. A tired woman drops bottles into cases, glass clinking, as a wrinkled janitor clang-clangs stacking chairs into piles, all seemingly before the last chords have ceased ringing or the dancers stopped dancing. The caretaker, a toothpick jutting from the dark seam of his mouth, builds the stacks and slides them across the powdered floor to a crawl space beneath the stage. Sherri is gone.

Twila and Trask tug on coats and cross the wooden floor sleepily, holding hands. Amp lights glow red. The guitarist rubs a blue cloth sensuously up and down the neck and fret-board of his Fender. The drummer switches off his snare, takes the set down. Bottles and glasses litter the amps and the foot of the stage. "You guys are good," says a young kid, face buttered with acne, "do you have a video?" A pretty Indian woman, a vivid scarlet rose held in her sleek black hair, perches on the edge, chewing gum. Bye bye, she says to some cowboys.

Outside the hall cars slide into the wind, into each other, ice shining under them. Trask and Twila huddle into their coats and stride quickly along the avenue to the trolley stop. Walls of snow form a barrier down the centre of the avenue, gritty snow and sand ploughed higher and higher over an endless winter. The road surface is polished pearl-white by the passage of wind and tires, the lawns buried, all leaves long ago stripped and smothered. Twila and Trask hug until the trolley rattles to a halt, her blouse warm to touch under her thick jacket. They clamber into the warmth of the bus, huddle close on a seat. Light glitters on the snow, bends.

Twila lives close to the cathedral in a beautiful Queen Anne. They slip under the arched door. "They're tearing the house down," she says, dabbing balm on his cracked lips, laughing at his drunken attempts to pucker. "We got the notice at Christmas."

"You're kidding. Why?"

"Bigger parking lot for Acme Novelty." Twila plays Schubert on a scratchy mono machine. Trask can't relax.

"This fucking town. Knocks everything down, the old courthouse, the post office tower. . . ."

"Janis Joplin's drink," she says, pouring him Southern Comfort. They neck in the kitchen then she leads him by the hand to her bedroom. From her window sash he can see McDougal's Funeral Parlour. He closes his eyes as she lifts one foot to a chair to place her diaphragm.

Bodies look white in the winter light and now she is cold under his nervous fingers, breath sawing, springs creaking like the poplar branch clawing at the frosted pane and he rolls from her on the cool sheets, tense, held back by something. The clock glows orange past her in dim blue light.

"It doesn't matter. It's nice being with someone." She moves close on the quilted comforter. "This is nice."

"I should head out," and Trask swings his legs over the high edge of her bed. Tired, he untangles his long johns from his crumpled jeans and yanks them on, deciding there are few things less romantic than thermal underwear.

Twila sees him to the arched door, shivering and looking younger still in a slip she has put on.

"Why don't you stay?"

"I should head out."

"Don't forget this." She runs off and returns with the mickey and a note with her phone number. She kisses him goodnight, years between them.

"Call me," she says.

"Get to bed before you catch a death."

Her porch light flicks off and Trask trudges the snow-packed walk to the Avenue, stopping by a car lot to hitchhike. Vision seems sharpened by the intense cold. "I am insane," he says. Breath blossoms as he swallows Southern Comfort, humming *Me And Bobby McGee*, staring at the acre of frozen cars, the funeral home, the Catholic hospital, the white curtains and leaded panes of her bedroom window. No traffic, the dead of night.

"I should have stayed," he says, thinking of her slim legs curving from the fringe of the slip. He paces the snow, stamping his feet, banging his boots together. His toes hurt already, ears and nose stinging in the freezing air. Too cold to snow.

The lights of the intersection click from green to yellow to red over and over and over. Inside stiff gloves he bunches his fingers into fists to keep them from freezing as the blood retreats from the extremities.

Trask calculates the number of blocks to walk to the west. It is too far: I have to get a ride. Up the block the window seems to watch him. Ornate hands glow on the funeral chapel clock. Trask wonders who is dying in the hospital, ready for the long walk through the clicking lights to the funeral home. Another swig of Comfort: purge the ghosts at the crosswalk.

Finally headlights, thumb raised, a rusted MG Midget stopping. Trask runs to the car, discomfort and irritation evaporating with a ride. He eases down into the low-slung seat, its cold leather crackling. The Midget jerks forward with a clunking sound, a tooth perhaps chipped or missing on first gear. The moustached driver seems intent on ignoring the sound.

"Must be freezing out there."

"Really," Trask replies automatically.

"This can be a cold town," the driver says with great seriousness. The roof of the little car is lined up with a thick grey blanket. He scrapes at the windshield to clear it of frost.

"English heaters don't work worth a damn. Not made for this climate."

"Which way you headed?" asks Trask.

"Oh, I don't know." The driver laughs nervously. "Just driving around, killing time. Couldn't sleep," he adds with his eyes clamped straight ahead. He is a few years older than Trask. CKUA is tuned in on the static-buzzed radio, some old blues. They drive west past Betty's Lunch, cowboys and Indians and oil rig roughnecks fighting on the sidewalk. "Get a load of that," says the driver. "This place is the Balkans."

They drive. Streets they pass now are emptied, Verna Beaver's Coiffures and Mr. Submarine throwing light for no one, muffled barrelhouse piano and blues harp on the car speakers, air outside looking grained, grey. They pass ravines leading to the river, crescents above, hedges; cross an ancient bridge, its concrete bones brown, cracked.

"This corner will be fine."

The driver gears down, makes the corner and clunk-clunk-clunks up the elm-lined street. "I'll take you to your place." The headlights brush each trunk, each tree carved from rough china, limbs like pointing skeletons under the Victorian streetlamps, sap held back forced underground. In front of the railroad house the driver reefs on the emergency brake, turns, air dark behind his head. A nylon hangs from a limb. "Would you like to make some money?"

Trask opens the car door.

"I'd love to give you a blow job," the driver breathes in a sad even tone, gloved hand vibrating on the gear shift.

Trask attempts to imagine himself exchanging seats, driving with a man's mouth on him, taking cash.

"Listen," he says, "thanks for the ride," he says, "I appreciate it," he says.

Trask moves up the walk, air knifing into his lungs, his clothes. On each side snow is banked chest high where he has shovelled it into bevelled dikes and high walls. The Midget's engine revs, jerks the red car sideways in the icy passage, whipping a quick U-turn and speeding past, the driver headed downtown again through the outstretched branches and balustrades of snow.

On the kitchen table are gloves and a note. Cigarettes. Trask recognizes Carson's writing on the note but is not interested in her latest from the world of positive thinking. He pulls at his boots, stamping snow on the linoleum.

Carson sleeps in Trask's small bed, blond hair spread over the blue linen. He looks at her, her tweed skirt hung over a desk chair, touches her blouse and brassiere. She sleeps breathing faintly.

He finishes the mickey and a bag of gingersnaps, watches a Fred Astaire film on television. What would it be like to dance like that? Are these dancers dead now? A bit player resembles Sid the bouncer. "Stop me if I become morose," the character says to Fred Astaire.

"You bet Sid," replies Trask. They do a dance number involving mops. Trask imagines the actors after the day's shooting is done. Going home exhausted or cruising rainbow-hued autos beneath the shaggy palms and hard sun of 1940s Hollywood. Operators are standing by, speaks the television personality. Then nothing shows but religious messages, national anthems, Indian-head test patterns and finally furious snow behind the blue cathode tube.

In England they are up already. Even in Newfoundland, fishermen starting up the engines across the continent, leaving their wives and slipping into the dark waters before dawn. Perhaps he will call in sick tomorrow, perhaps Twila will meet him at the Luncheonette for French toast and Earl Grey, maybe things will happen with him and Twila this winter. "Call me," she said.

After turning out every light, he makes his way like a blind man to the bedroom.

"Who's there," asks Carson in the dark. "Is that you?"

He stands on the cold tiles, pretends he is in the mouth of a swift river: he is young and seeing how long he can stand it.

"Is that you baby? Why don't you answer?"

His chest moves up and down, his eyes get used to it. He stares into the dark, into the long season, trying to see what he has come here for, to take his losses with a gambler's grace, a poker face, no regrets. Later he could hate her.

"Did your rugby player disappoint?"

"You son of a bitch."

"That's it," he says, opening his shirt, listening to the buttons find their way to strange corners of the room.

"You prick," she whispers, nearly crying.

"Now you're getting close," he whispers back. "Now you're getting warm."

Dancing Nightly in the Tavern

The horse surges sideways to fill Luke's vision. He feels the heat of its sides, reads the nicks in its winter coat, rolls from the hooves and fetlocks he had been checking, in the corner of his swimming eye sees Woody's skinny shadow climb the buckskin from the fence, sees as if from underwater, thinking, *no, ride the pinto, this fucker's not been rid all winter.*

Woody laughing: "He's a wooly sonuvabitch!"

"Crazy bastard," mutters Luke, Woody rocking above, sky the colour of ice, Woody on the back, dark against the sky, strands of light, horsehair on the wire, Woody laughing like before the deaths, until his leg is raked down the barbwire tearing denim and skin, his face clenched, twisted mouth cursing, eyes furious. The gouged flesh open, visible, as the frayed white threads soak to pink.

"You hammer-headed cocksucker," hisses Woody, pounding the horse's big head, pulling the reins back until the buckskin's yellow-green teeth are bared to the slobbery bit.

The horse dances backwards, head erect, refusing to clear

the fence, rump lowered, then hind hooves floating up in clods of wet ground and smashing back. The horse can smell him.

Luke pushes the wall of flesh, shoving it finally from the barbs, the shot strands of light and black hair caught, the buckskin rearing, Woody scrambling in the mane and hooves slam to earth, Woody's teeth clamping with a click, eyes closed and head rolling, snapping. The gelding contorts impossibly, heaving Woody off balance, one arm waving as if in greeting. The hind legs kick out, the back up and Woody is free into the air over the Austin-Healey and flooded summerfallow.

Luke picks up the hat, hands it to Woody. The horse smells it on Woody, Luke knows.

Woody limping to the car, his bottle. "You ever want to de-nut that fucker, let me know," he says, taking a swig.

"It's a gelding." The buckskin tongues the blue salt lick innocently, but a glare in the eye betrays it.

WHY WOULD ANYONE put a well in such low ground, wonders Luke. The bucket drags up streaming water, full of bottles of Calgary Export, his hand cold tugging the rope, the freezing metal handle. Luke pours water into the claw foot bathtub that serves as a trough for the horses. The water is dirty with spring runoff. Woody hugs the beaded bottles to his chest, limps uphill to the crooked cabin with Luke trailing, shoves his shoulder into the door, swearing as it scrapes over the crooked wooden floor, a blond arc cut in the dirt-coloured planks.

Woody paws a pack of matches, lights up, coughs the first jawful into his closed fist. Leans back in the wooden chair, smoke shrouding his face, thuds his cowboy boots on the sill of dead flies.

Luke finds the Mercurochrome and Woody winces even before it is applied to the wound. A torn shirt for wrapping. Woody's head twists in the jacket's sheepskin, checking out the tiny cabin and, through the grimy window, the yard; the mess of the flooded drive, the pickup with glass kicked in by a stallion, the rusting tractor and harrow. The stands of tamarack he knew are gone, cut into fenceposts.

HIS MICKEY OF FIVE STAR whiskey is finished now, the sardine can crammed with butts, no filters, smoked to the ends. Luke fries eggs and beans on top of the wood stove, iron clanging loudly against iron. Woody swallows his food noisily, nearly choking, broken yolks running into the beans' brown sauce, a bead of yellow caught on his chin. With both hands he grips the emptied plate like a steering wheel and licks a pale tongue over the grooved surface.

"How are the oil rigs?" asks Luke.

Woody thrusts up a hand missing two fingers in answer. The hand stained the shade of the gelding's teeth. The fire snaps as they feed planks into the stove's belly.

"Money's good." He sucks his smoke. "I could get you on. You want to get on? I could get you on."

"Save much?" asks Luke.

Woody shakes his head with a bit of a snort, laughing smoke from his nostrils. "Spend exactly what I clear. Hit town with a grand and leave without a pot to piss in." He leans back. "You get hooked," he says, peering around as if for someone else, dragging dirty fingers through his curly hair.

"Didn't you have a job?" he asks Luke.

"I had a job." Working the summer and sere fall fighting

fires with the Indians on the eastern slopes. When it got colder, the Indians stopped setting the fires and Luke was out of work. Woody opens another bottle.

Luke steps outside to the horses, the silhouette of the barn-shaped cabin leaning starkly in last light. A red-tailed hawk spirals the burnt stubble south of the cabin. Blackbirds harass the hawk, forcing it to the ground. Luke stares at the red-tail, the horse, its winter fat. Should be more fun trying to get a saddle on that broom-tail, he thinks.

"Long time since I've been on a horse," says Woody inside. "Bad winter. Damn near froze my ass off this winter."

"Same as always," says Luke.

"I don't know, seemed colder."

In the flat light Woody's flesh resembles dead wood. "Swear I'm going to quit these damn things."

At midnight Luke scrapes the chair back to stand.

"Stay up a while," says Woody, his eyes unfocused. "Come on. Stay a bit." The cabin creaks around them. Under the imitation grey-brick siding are the original logs, contracting, settling into the clay. The cabin is over one hundred years old, the cellar once used by rustlers to hide beef, a dirty rug now over the trap door.

Luke lays a mattress on the living room floor for Woody. Two blankets. As Luke lies in his loft he can hear bats scrabble in the rafters and walls.

A LOUD THUMP. Light glows from the kitchen. Woody, pitched from the rocker, lies on the floor, mouth parted a fraction, breath whistling in his nostrils. Cigarette burns scar the white table and floorboards around him. He takes a vague swing at Luke as he tries to rouse him. His lined face as grey as the tamarack posts they dragged in and burned. Luke attempts to drag him under the arms to the mattress. Scythes of sweat soak the armpits of Woody's jean shirt.

"Christ you weigh a ton." Luke gives up, wraps the cowhide around him where he lies.

Later Luke wakes in the darkness, a cowboy boot cuffing his face, the close smell of roughout suede, Woody rolling into the bed, Woody's head at Luke's feet, Woody's belt and pants bunched at his ankles, caught there by his boots.

"For Christ's sake Woody. Sleep on the fucking mattress!"

Woody grunts, swears in reply. Luke moves against the cold wall as far as he can. Later Woody falls from the cot. The shirt-strip bandage tinged red. Again Luke swathes him in the cowhide, adding a striped Hudson's Bay blanket around his shoulders. "You sorry bugger."

LUKE WAKES AFTER DAWN, Woody is up already, perched coughing on the purple couch. He wears only a shirt, unbuttoned, his eyes squeezed shut, head and chest shaking, a fist clenched to his lips, rocking as if still on the buckskin. Between coughing fits he gazes blankly into corners, white skinny legs apart, the one bandaged, the shadow of hair under the shirt tails, his cock shrunken.

It is too cold to get up, decides Luke in his blankets. He hears the truck start up, but sinks back into sleep.

Slashed plastic beats at the glass. Using the dipper, Luke drinks from the water bucket, then fills the wash basin. Half-stunned flies buzz in the soapy water, graze the dirty plates and silver. Luke rubs cold water into his face, fingers his hair back.

Shadowed with several nights' beard, Woody's face glares from the doorway; dark and white skin puffy, the inexact shade of the cloud cover.

"How'd ya sleep?" Luke asks, bending to peer in the tiny cracked mirror.

"Bad. Wake up sick and can't get back to sleep. Lie there waiting." He sits, then gets up, paces. "The guy at the camp did some tests." He picks up a *Western Horseman*, glances at the blue cover and then chucks it. "I'm supposed to be in Charles Camsell right now but fuck if I'm going to lay round some friggin' hospital and get poked at. . . ." Woody walks to the cold stove, arms tight around his chest.

"Cold?" asks Luke. Camsell is the TB hospital in the city, he thinks, Indians mainly. Fifteen to a smoky shack; them and TB are like that.

"Fucking freezing," says Woody, wiping his nose on his sleeve, trailing a dark stripe on the denim cuff. The air pink under the clouds in the distance. "Just might clear up."

Down past the well the horses scratch at a last bit of snow. Woody cradles a half gallon from the Austin-Healey, pours wine in two teacups.

Luke wanders onto the porch, a breeze in his damp hair. His pickup is backed up to the porch, a small freezer in the back. Woody walks out, a grin cut ear to ear.

"Stole it, off a stoop. Some mobile home other side of Max Solbrekken's Bible Camp." He chuckles but it foams into a cough somewhere between his throat and mouth.

"Well kid, you said . . . you said you like your beer nearly froze."

Hands in his pockets, Woody spits into the hedge, leaning

on one wall as Luke opens the freezer. Inside are frozen loaves of homemade bread, whitefish from Pigeon Lake, packages of moose, beef and venison—their brown wrapping labelled with felt pen. A woman's handwriting. Luke thinks of her detailed work, her time, the pen and butcher paper. He climbs behind the freezer and pushes it easily from the truck to the porch wall.

Woody plucks two T-bones from the freezer. "Dinner," he announces formally, holding the meat aloft like a trophy, his chest shaking in his shirt.

CLOUD BANKS BULGE, PORCELAIN. A slate-blue goshawk, male, clings to a dead willow. A rank of aspens and willows shake in a windbreak around three sides of the Conjuring Creek Cemetery, bark on the trunks cropped by deer. Branches form cracks in the sky, reminding Luke of the inside of his parents' china teapot. Woody drinks wine. Magpie and hawk nests hang in the higher boughs.

Luke points out the truck window to the back of the graveyard.

"Saw a lynx in there Christmas day."

"That a fact."

"Lot of deer this winter."

Tiny white fences hug some of the graves. Flowers sprawl on two recent Cree suicides. Crooked and chipped stones are scattered like broken teeth across the clearing. Most have simple crosses.

"You got a lady?" Woody asks, scratching his chest between buttons. Where one pearl button is gone, a safety pin hooks his shirt together.

"No. They all get knocked up by high school. Or they fuck off to the city."

Condensation beads on the insides of the cracked glass, shivers down the window in rivulets. Woody traces his name with a yellow finger, then rubs it out.

"I always meant to put flowers on theirs," Luke says, nodding into the graveyard. "Seemed like the thing to do."

"I guess."

"Never knew where to get any though."

Smoke from Woody's cigarette drifts into Luke's nostrils. Clouds wreathe Woody, reminding Luke of the bushfires fought in the hills above Brule.

"Yablonski's burnt. Watched all that booze go up."

"Where's he now?"

"Motel."

"You drink all those?" Woody pointing to the plastic stars taken from Five Star bottles and pasted on the dash. "You drink those?"

"Nah. Took them off old bottles in the yard. I liked the way they looked on your dashboard."

"Yeah, but . . . that's not the point. You drink them and then you can put the star up."

"Okay, I'll take them off."

"Don't bother now. Hey, leave them, kid leave them."

Luke peels the gold plastic stars and hurls them into the ditch, leaves the window down and stares out, breathing in cold solid air. Woody finishes the wine, then brings beer up from the back of the truck. He opens two on his belt buckle and hands one to Luke as a peace offering.

"You wanna look at the graves or anything?"

"Nah, let's just sit."

They sit. The windshield is spidered with cracks spread to all corners of the glass by gravel back roads and long freezes. Things get brittle, shook up. Things fall apart, thinks Luke.

Dusk falls and they stare into the dark windshield. Luke counts the bumps on the bottle, noting how many times it has been shipped back to the brewery in Edmonton. Five and they smash it, he is told. Hank wonders who else has emptied this bottle.

Headlights flare in the rear-view and Woody turns, the seat creaking beneath him.

"Head her out. Might be my friends the Mounties." Woody rolls his window down quickly and throws the bottle over the top of the cab toward the opposite ditch. The bottle shatters against the wooden stock racks, raining glass in the headlights. "Damn, forgot the stock racks."

Luke drives down the All-Weather Road, past the old creamery and turns off overlooking Empty Creek. After the truck is shut off, the engine chugs violently. Luke keeps a boot hard on the brake pedal and lets the clutch out. The motor stops with a jerk.

"You did some time?" Luke asks.

"In the Fort. Got picked up running smoke from Vancouver." He sits staring straight ahead. Fuckers must've set me up." His mouth a level slit, a crack in dry kindling.

"What's it like?"

"The Fort? Fuck. Like anywhere else, its own little world. Fun if you like guys and tattoos. Hey kid, is that town cop, what's-his-face, still around?"

"No. RCMP took over all the smaller places. They cruise

by every Thursday. We all behave on Thursday." Luke carries more beer up to the cab. "Want to check out town?"

"Just sit," Woody mumbles, a smoke between wooden lips.

After the case is gone they decide to go in after all, to pick up more beer at the hotel.

Moths spit lazily into the lure of their headlights as the pickup rumbles down the Correction Line, the moon steaming from a cloud, shining, a chrome hubcap rolling from a car wash. The marquee on the hotel states: Black Stallion Hotel—Dancing Nitely in Tavren.

"Learn to fuckin' spell," comments Woody. "Hey, I didn't tell you about my new gun. Guy in Oregon made it for me. Does nice work."

They tramp across the ugly tavern to buy a cold case, staring into the noisy farmers and Indians, into the dusty mirrors. Woody forces money on Luke for the beer. The touch of the barmaid's hand giving Luke the change. Luke looking back at her as they leave.

A crowd is circled in the gravel. Walking by they hear breathing, blows and grunts, someone's heavy fall and the dance going on; drunk boots kicking the gut, the head, *pock-pock* like blows on a rotten melon. Three older farmers pull the big guy away and a skinny kid lies face up in a pool of yellowish puke with swirls of blood in it. One eye looks broken open.

Woody yanks Luke's arm hard, drags him to the truck, the rough edge of the beer case banging Luke's thigh. They hear the skinny kid is up from Ontario. Looking for work on the oil patch.

"Stupid fuckers." The moon wobbles in the clouds, a vacant socket.

"You used to fight a lot," Luke says. Woody is small but tough, what is called wiry.

"Used to," cracking open the fresh case. Hunches in the cab fuming smoke and sweat, inhaling half a bottle in a swallow, half a cigarette with a furious drag. "Get me out of here."

Woody breaks Luke's favourite chair. They are Indian leg wrestling on the floor of the cabin, lying flat, head to feet, raising one straightened leg once, twice, a third time and locking it around the opponent's thigh. Luke flips him over to win and stands, off guard.

Woody pushes him. Luke lands hard on the chair and the legs splay, collapse, both of them yelling like idiots, mouths open without a bottle. Luke stands shouting and Woody shoves him once more and Luke's boot breaks through his father's old gut-string guitar, Woody stomping out to the car with Luke after him trying to shake the splintered guitar from his foot.

Outside the rising sun is crooked and red and Woody's Austin-Healey revs and shakes free of the mudhole where the driveway was last fall.

Luke watches the slate-blue car disappear. He blinks into the new sun, his cats chasing cabbage moths that flutter between their paws from the dew-damp clover. Tosses the guitar on the porch roof, hearing the engine for a minute after the sports car has slipped from view.

AFTER THE GROUND HAS THAWED and the transmission gone Luke rides the gelding into town; pay some bills, pick up a few things at the Co-op and Wilson's IGA. Luke had hired on at the gravel pit, running the crusher for two weeks, but the truck's tranny seized and he had no wheels. Had to quit. There was a promise of overtime. Dumb luck, he thinks.

The gelding is no problem; it knows Luke, the sure smell. His legs.

The store is dim, low ceiling and pine floorboards. Wilson thinks Luke has to know already, fills in a crony, an insurance man in a hunting jacket.

"Two bouncers up there in Grande Cache. Kicked the shit out of him and threw him through a couple picture windows they got in the new mall there."

Luke moves in the aisle as if hit with a rope. Turns to listen. The insurance man shakes his head, places a pinch of Red Chief in his jaw. The grocer's soft hands tally the sales, ring up the measly cans of tuna, the Kraft Dinner.

"Kid, I'm real sorry," he says.

Luke bites from a stale Oh Henry!, looks around. There is no taste to the chocolate. The store smells of aged wood, polish, Ukrainian sausage.

"Those two fellows been up before the judge before," Wilson continues. "Mark my words, if they don't get it good this time." The grocer looks up from behind his apron at Luke walking outside into the light. "Don't you worry," the grocer calls, still sticking Luke's order in a cardboard box.

Luke buys a sealer jar of homebrew from Yablonski, the displaced bootlegger, at his new quarters in the Sail-Inn Motel. Room zero. They sit drinking as the town's clapboard streets ease into streaked darkness.

Luke steals into one of the grocer's cars after midnight, a repossessed Chev. The ignition protrudes and can be turned by hand without a key. Off you go. Yablonski promises to take the gelding back to Luke's corral in his GMC. Driving north Luke leaves the last farms, enters scrub pine.

BY DAWN LUKE WHEELS into Woody's last camp, an ugly clearing of trailers and 4 X 4 crewcabs. Roughnecks wander muskeg in crusted jackets, clutching gloves and hard hats, looking too tired to stare, coveralls blotched in slime blown from the drill's shaft.

A foreman is in a tiny office drinking coffee. He gives Luke a final pay slip, some cash and letters, and a battered horsehide grip, bound by binder twine. Wind rocks the panelled trailer. Luke drinks black coffee, signs the papers for the paymaster, gives away the Chev.

The Austin-Healey is stalled in gumbo to the axles and oil pan. The foreman waves a D-9 over to haul the car to solid ground. The bulldozer clanks over the muskeg, blue-black smoke jetting from twin stacks above the earmuffed operator. The exhaust system tears away as the car is dragged.

"Woody worked for me for years!" shouts a toolpush, leaning over Luke in the Healey's low driver's seat. The engine idles high, deafening without a muffler. "He was a good worker," the toolpush shouts. Some words are lost. "Fell off a triple rig onto his head. Sonuvabitch walked away! You want on the oil patch, no sweat. Ask for Carl!" he finally yells, slapping the muscled fender. The name RUDY is taped on the front of his hard hat.

Luke cannot keep his eyes open. "What about these bouncers?" Luke asks. The wind everywhere, another season imposed over the muddy muskeg.

"Legal channels, let's say." The man leans. "Son, I know

you're itching. One question: you going to fuck over yourself because of this? It'll be taken care of." He leans even closer, stubble nearly brushing Luke's face. "You should've been here few nights back. Woody's Newfie buddies had one of their wakes. Man oh man. Sat up all night drinking screech and tore up the bunkhouse so bad we had to haul the thing right the fuck out." His eyes look sad, crazed, but Luke cannot decide if the man is affected by the loss of Woody or the trailer. Luke stomps the gas to the floor.

It is cold and loud driving the Healey. Luke kills a mickey of Five Star he finds in the suitcase. The horsehide reminds Luke of Woody struggling to stay on the gelding. There is also the heavy pistol Woody spoke of, a .45 bored out to take a .410 shotgun shell. With some flame and smoke it can punch eighteen holes in a door or fender. An illegal gun and Luke doesn't much like it; it affects the balance of things. It could be handy, he thinks. The radio plays Lawrence Welk crooning *Life Is A Holiday On Primrose Lane.*

"Like fuck it is," the bottle thrown against the dials. The radio quits with snapping sounds, broken glass littering the dash, the seats, Luke's lap. He laughs. "Cracking up," he says.

Steering with one hand he leans to retrieve the gold star, accidentally cutting his index finger on the chunk of glass it is attached to. The car veers from side to side between the ditches, drifts as he peels the star from the shard of glass, sticks the star on the dashboard, a bubble of blood on one point.

Looking at the star, the road, Luke realizes he has Woody's bottle, his car, his pistol; he glances in the mirror expecting Woody's face. The same blue eyes. Legal channels! Jesus. Who will take care of it if not me?

Luke drives fast thinking, I don't know that I can kill some joker even with what they have done to someone close, family, but there is a clear need to get even, eye for a fucking eye. He has never felt what it is to be a coward. He tries hard to imagine what Woody would have done back before he was sick or what he would have Luke do now, and Luke doubts they are one and the same thing.

It is some miles to the T intersection where Luke must turn one way or the other. He wants to stop in a bar for coffee, a beer, pick a fight, pick up a woman, anything but there's nothing here. Except for a pull to the side, Woody's Austin-Healey seems to pilot itself, the slate-blue machine unmuffled and powerful around the heir. Lobstick pines loom green-yellow, the same shade as the horse's teeth, as Woody's fist. The blurred trees line the only road cut over ridges of lodgepole and tamarack; the scaly conifers climbing right back up with the purple fireweed after each cyclic stripping by winter or seasons of fire.

Night of Blue Weeds

LADIES NIGHT declares a blue poster upon the tin door, Fatman Memphis & His Rockabilly Rebels playing wildly on the tiny stage the strippers used before the Catholic Women's League ran them back into the swamps.

Mote Carver, on his first Heilemans, on his first cheque from unemployment, watches the band with his mind on other things. Two or three weeks, they said at the Palmetto Fruit Co., a month at the outside, then they'll rehire some drivers. This damn economy is killing me, Mote thinks. At least no one has died on me. I have lost my job and my Ford Fairlane and fine things but no one has died on me yet.

"My wife and my car I lost down in Quauhnahuac," he says out loud. "I have needs," he says. The barkeep, a filthy towel knotted to his belt loop, rocks back and forth on Cuban heels, and Mote cannot tell if the man is listening.

Jenna Jane, a friend of a friend from North Carolina, touches Mote on the shoulder as she silently passes.

"There were ornate churches there," he continues, as if to her. "I could not get home."

"How many miles on the car?" asks the bartender, but Mote is staring at the woman who has touched his shoulder and passed, her hand a pale fossil resting now on some other man's purple sweater.

Mote understands he wants her, wishes her to speak in his ear with her lips close, her hand, pale as butter, on him. Yet the effort.

Mote studies Jenna Jane's hair, the sweep of her hand easy over the man's back, his ear turned casually to her pink lips. Her curves perfect as the saxophone. Mote tries to remember if she knows his wife, wonders where his wife is.

The rockabilly saxophonist honks another wild-eyed solo, arching his neck to swing the gleaming horn above his head and into the glare of the orange and pink spots, the instrument a brass question mark sprouting from his soft mouth. Clutching angular Fenders, the twanging guitarists jump around the stage in string ties and padded shoulders, shuddering atop amplifiers and the piano, coiffured pompadour wedges unaffected by their frenetic gyrations. The smaller guitarist madly works his tremolo bar, an acid-induced vision of Buddy Holly: sparkling horn-rims and a foot-high quiff of rooster-red hair greased upward and outward in the shape of an aircraft carrier.

Couple after couple stream in now past Mote, Ladies Free, the band hot, packing in a crowd, everyone with someone, dancing like lunatics. Drinking alone, Mote thinks, thinks I am golden man in the midst of dank and cigarettes and swamps. I must go soon, before the malaise sets in. He sips and counts his change, calculating how many drinks he can swing with this silver and whether that number will suffice.

Mote looks again to Jenna Jane. She is dancing now, entranced by the curly-haired sax player; he's swinging his horn, he's got the big horn, but flings it aside at the end of the solo leaping down to dance with the nearest women. The young men dancing with them continue, but nervously, glancing with puzzlement at their now sluggish feet and ugly hands, comparing themselves with the manic horn man, the pale star who finally returns to the stage to play, eyes shut into pink light, wrenching at the saxophone with his mouth and hands as if to tear the instrument apart key by key.

The next number is languid and the saxman lowers himself to the edge of the stage, long legs crossed, playing smoothly to the women, eyeing them from under his curls until the two men give up dancing and sit down, pissed off, defeated. The two women remain, dancing near each other but facing only the player. What has happened to things, to the old pairings? Mote swings on the bar stool to look elsewhere, to ignore this Darwinism on the dance floor.

FARTHER BACK: a pool shark kneels at a slate table, as if a priest at an altar, to rack up the balls. Citizens of the republic poke a man in the ass with the butt ends of pool cues. The man giggles nervously as the pokes get more and more vicious and he is forced to dance higher and higher to minimize their effect. Mote swivels again, turns meditative.

MOTE'S PHILOSOPHICAL QUESTION of the hour: Why don't women ever buy men drinks? He mulls this studying a beautiful couple, *the* beautiful couple, dance to *Sea Cruise*, their perfect silhouettes erect in the pool table glare, the man tall, in a flesh-coloured shirt and white zoot-suit replete with chain. She dances cooly, straight, pearl earrings at her lobes, a string of pearls obedient on her breasts, her thick hair bouncing in a wholesome blond ponytail that hangs at the back of her red dress. "Oo-wee, oo-wee babee," hollers the singer.

Mote intoxicated, slightly divorced from it all, thinks again on the state of the economy, while noticing that the cheap clothes he was forced to buy in Mexico after the thefts are falling to pieces now. "Comeonletmetakeyouona—SEACRUISE!"

Two men rush onto the dance floor, one still sucking a cigarette and beginning to dance before he has stopped running, whipping one slim arm in fast circles, his partner thrusting an arm up like a power salute, in time, knees flexing and hips grinding. Both wear tight scarlet pants and have eye makeup and slightly spiked hair. The dance floor fills with micro-minis, leather and chains, Brylcreem ducktails, granny glasses, porkpie hats and skinny ties, Nazi gear; half a dozen eras and retro movements flaunted. There has to be some irony, thinks Mote, that this is all to the accompaniment of music made originally for Memphis greaseballs and Arkansas rednecks.

As he walks to the washroom, Mote has sombre thoughts on the future of youth, the nature of his credit rating, the foothills of the brooding Sierra Madre Oriental, his lost Ford Fairlane, the bouncing cheques.

INSIDE THE WASHROOM two men appear to be necking. The closest turns to Mote with a slight tilt of his face. He drops his partner, who cracks his head loudly on a porcelain fixture.

"Say Tim," the first man says to Mote, ignoring the prone figure.

"My name is not Tim," replies Mote. "What is with your pal?"

"No. Say Tim."

"Tim. Tim. Jesus Tim!"

"You say it funny too. Anyway, if you must know he is so intoxicated I think his heart stopped. I've given him mouth to mouth several times. I'm worried he's no longer with us. And he is not my pal."

Mote could not tell if he was dead or not. The only dead he had viewed were in car wrecks and pine coffins.

"Please leave us," the man says, giving Mote several twenties from a roll of cash.

A TABLE AT THE EDGE of the dance floor. Mote asks three women sitting by themselves if they would care to dance.

"No."

"No?"

"No."

"Wrinkles," Mote hears one whisper as he turns. He pushes his way to the stool, wanting to appear as if this latest in a series of rejections means nothing.

Jenna Jane, the woman who touched his shoulder, grabs him from behind and leads him to the dance floor. Does she like him? Mote feels she will seize on anyone to remain in the lights, in view of the curly-haired sax player. The second woman is still there, dancing frantically in the hope of sleeping with a band member. Is there a male equivalent to this? Mote wonders.

Mote dances dutifully with his new partner, Jenna Jane shaking her head, her hair, her arms, her everything. She grasps her skirt with two hands, sashaying it about her to reveal glimpses of milk thighs and apparently unclad shadows between. Be cool, Mote cautions himself, be the serpent under the flower, for women have radar when it comes to desperation. Jenna Jane's substantial breasts do not stir despite her best efforts. It is something to see.

To communicate, Mote grasps her warm arm and shouts at the side of her head. The contact with skin and hair, her eyes, the side of her bosom by his hand; he is aroused. He clutches at her and they cease dancing as he forces his tongue at her mouth, nearly falling as they French kiss for a few moments, but she pushes him away, upset, and dances again, an embarrassed glance in the direction of the man with the horn.

"Keep it clean, okay?" she says.

"Yes Ma'am. It's the economy." A saxophone lurking.

"I swear all men are fucked up."

"Well, some more so than others." So this is permanence.

Mote struggles to resume shuffling his cheap Mexican shoes, but he is too self-conscious; the moves seem suddenly, clearly, absurd. In near-paralysis, he has to think out every step or turn. He returns to his perch.

Mote has several Heineken, a treat courtesy of the man in the restroom. Mote feels better with the money glowing in his pockets, there is comfort there. The saxophonist vibrates his head to squeeze a final note and yells "Don't go 'way folks!" Feedback squeals in the amps as he bounds from the stage and drops panting on a stool beside Mote. Mote tries to remember if he has eaten, if he has food at home other than FlavorKist Saltines and generic peanut butter.

You were great, man, great, man! says the bartender, sliding scotch on the rocks. You were great man! agrees everyone who can get close. Mote entertains feelings of claustrophobia. The horn player holds court for a few minutes, looks Mote over while sipping at his scotch. Takes dental pieces from his talented mouth and starts playing with Mote's leg, clamping the wet gums and teeth to his thigh.

Everyone laughs at the star and his jokes—he's great man!—and Mote has to laugh too, thinks *he's young for false teeth*, knocks him from the bar stool, one clean one and flat out down the stairs two at a time.

Jealousy is a terrible thing, he thinks outside. I hope I didn't damage his mouth. Or is that trumpet players?

Mote looks up the street, up at the stars, and is reminded of driving to the observatory in the hills south of town. His wife knew the astronomer boarding there. No hamlets near the observatory, no farms or lights, perfect, the young scientist told them, this is the darkest place, the darkest place in Blackhawk county. The three of them drained can after can of Falstaff at the bumper of the car, Theolonius Anton blowing a cool tenor on the car radio.

No, thinks Mote now, the man with the telescope has no monopoly on darkness. There are other dark places and Mote understands he has talent for finding them.

Leaves blow past, bits of veined leather. Mote studies the broken down rooming houses, their ugly flat-faced look, like frontier hotels, stairs a white zigzag down dark walls and yellow squares of light from the failed minarets.

Jenna Jane walks down the sidewalk from a car, twisting plastic from a new package of cigarettes. "Why did you sit down?" she says. "Why did you sit down? We were dancing," she says. "Have you seen my friend Rita?"

"Yes I have," lies Mote. "In the women's room even now, giving the pretty boy with the horn a blow job."

"Sure sure." She leaves him.

Mote counts his change for perhaps the eighteenth time, noticing now pink and blue loops of neon two blocks down, colours reflecting in the clean cars parked along the Rock Island tracks. The colours look good but blurred, for Mote is nearly blind in one eye. Amblyopia, the optometrist told him, have to catch it young. The glasses too were lost in Quauhnahuac. Mote gazes at the blurred colours of drinking, pure, all-consuming. He wishes he had a car for a drive along the Mississippi. He does some push-ups.

Jenna Jane returns to him near tears.

"She is, that bitch. I'm really sorry. I thought you were being mean."

"Well I was."

They walk a quarter of a block. "Yes and I guess some drunk asshole hit him in the mouth."

"No kidding," steering her into a cul-de-sac between old buildings, against a wall where they neck for a while, Mote pressing his hips cheaply against her.

"Not like this," and she leads Mote.

Funny, he thinks, considering how I loathed her only minutes ago, I'm eager for her now. Oh well, he decides, once you've been through your existential blue period what is left you but women? That and the false light of factories, of the Palmetto

Fruit Co., shacks on stilts, fists through the window and the word made flesh in a riverbank motel off Highway 61.

Jenna Jane leads Mote past the relicts of an orchard and across a playground, passing under the shadows and strange geometry of hewn cedar beams, nets and cages. Mote contemplates the sand, but no, Jenna Jane leads on to the Awry Powdermilk Bakery and the lane behind, to a warm air grate venting the ovens baking baguettes and crusty rolls through the night.

Mote lays his thick pea jacket on the grate, humming *Now I Lay Thee* religiously. Jenna Jane is insistent, hurry, hurry, and as he suspected, is without underwear. She wishes to rush but Mote is teasing, though this is not his usual way, searching lazily for her in the blue darkness with his mouth, brushing lips over the rise of hip bone jut, nuzzling down and into her with his tongue, the first taste different and then it doesn't taste, it is her and he is both in want and content, at the fountain.

Thanks, she whispers after, almost shyly, and she raises his head lightly with the tips of her fingers, as if it were a balloon, pulling him up, his face floating over the contours of her belly, her ribs and breasts, the hollow of her throat and her lips and as they kiss she guides his cock and the head is against her where she is soaking but tight and he moves against her lightly back and forth pushing and then it is that first feeling that is new each time, a miracle, his cock slides belonging there inside her muscles, born there with her sharp intake of breath and Mote feels in love, this boy is in love, even if he is only a replacement for the sax player, all that exists is to be rooted tight against her belly, her legs angling up at the sky in wonderful symmetry. Mote feels surprisingly hard, puzzlingly so. He works a hand beneath her and slips his smallest finger against her anus, slowly working it into her and she arches, her brow wrinkled and eyes concentrating as if to keep from crying so Mote asks if he is hurting her, do you want me to stop, he asks.

She looks at him as if noticing his presence for the first time, placing her fingers lightly on his bare ass to hold him close to her and doesn't speak for a moment and they can smell the loaves baking and feel warm air rising to their skin and she finally says, I don't want you to ever stop, with a silent laugh as if of exasperation and they continue, Jenna Jane coming against him in mid-air but Mote doesn't come, is again puzzled but pleased lying in the waft of heated air, as if perched on a tamed volcano.

It has never happened this way before. He will remember this: it is like drinking and drinking when he feels he is just about to unlock great secrets if he has more, it is coming to some greater understanding in the height above the tilt of her blue face in a spare light, about the words JESUS GOT THE POWER etched on a wall, about the circles and circles of blue weeds at the base of power poles reminding him of certain nights in Mexico, it is placing kisses on Jenna Jane's finger-tips and biting her lower lip, mistaking the sweep of an air-port beacon for heat lightning, amazed by the beauty of brick buildings he found ugly an hour earlier.

Mote comes finally at her house, with her in the shower, leaning in the white spray, mouths open, comes silent as a father and exhausted they fall over pulling down the shower curtain, ripping out its rings.

Pale mornings after, Mote chooses to ignore the slightly painful red sores at the base of his cock, knowing that he is the horn, that soon there will be work again at the Palmetto Fruit Co., that Mexico does not exist, that physical love is pure and perfect and there can be no ugliness or disease or dark places in Mote's home county.

Jesus Made Seattle Under Protest

Seventeen rides, seventeen rivers. They drive tilted streets past OK Loans, Cinema X, the tunnels of exhaust. The left lane closes and no one will let you in. "Where'd you learn to drive, Sesame St.!?" Ray Savitch senses a lesson: punish the slow, the ugly, those from out of town.

At sea level, Ray climbs from the snake-coloured Galaxie, thanks the driver. "Good luck," he says. Ray brushes his teeth in a Union '76 and spits blood with toothpaste, sink speckled, striking. Some days it gets hard to drag yourself from the puzzle of sheets.

Ray stands above a shore; squat ceaseless ferries bisecting the bay, white wakes like scar tissue, Warrior Peaks looming as salt heaps across dark blue chop.

Yachts heel, sails brushing sea. Portholed shanties perch a line between eelgrass and air. Pink boathouses yaw in sunlight, emitting snatches of hillbilly fiddle, the aroma of coho. A day that makes it worth the mildew.

Beneath sooty Alaskan Way a man strangles another. The

man stops and the two converse. He begins strangling him again. Then the rock to the head. The rising tide does not lift all boats.

The past spring things fell apart on the oil fields; a glut, the energy policy, shit and fan. They broke down the drilling derricks and trucked them south of the border to the Overthrust Belt of Wyoming and Montana, Ray given his pink slip, every guy and his dog given his pink slip. "That's all she wrote," the last driver slamming the Kenworth's black door in disgust.

Leases expire and are not renewed. Stepping from a Bauhaus highrise, Ray holds aloft his hand on the Yellowhead, to roll through magpies and mustard and silver poplar, to wend his way south and west from the oil patch boomtowns, from home and the thought of a winter without work, rising and falling across cordillera and glacial rivers and jack-leg fences holding dreamy-eyed cattle.

Like a shutter, clouds close for the rains of winter. Ray figures it out: his savings from roughnecking are gone, cash from picking apples and peaches in the hot valley gone, the pittance from working the cattle ranch in the Cariboo gone. It is Halloween, it is the sea, the sun and moon pulling tides in brainpan and vein, cock rising to ask what day and what month, seeking solace in red hearts and vaginas, in the distance to her navel, in going home. Toothless men swing off the Burlington Northern freights and ask for the on-ramp to Portland. Cherry Street. Studying women's shoes and hips.

Ray paid for his last woman at the Calgary Stampede, through the nose, an eventuality his immigrant parents failed to foresee in his Bible belt youth. Wearing silver shades, Ray Savitch put his cock to the planet and the planet rolled and opened under him, hinging to take the stove-hot idol within, working Ray into sleep after sleep, an anvil off a cliff, but still this business of price is like hairs in your peach cobbler.

Time was Ray strummed a Spanish guitar, had a two-bedroom with a view of the river, had a thirty-year-old Buick, two-door, red with a white roof. En route to the Ma-Me-O dance, Ray rolled the Buick in the fields of spring. Sneeze and it's laid it in a corner of green oats, whitewalls spinning. The apartment and Spanish guitar fell away similarly. Now what? is his question. According to Immigration he is an alien. The unions have the docks.

On Occidental, a man stops Ray.

"My name is Howard T. Melville from Chicago, Illinois." He speaks very quickly, lifting a long brown finger to Ray's chest. "I need to call my mama. Can you hep me please with a single dollar?"

Ray laughs at him. "You're asking me?" There are scars at the man's eyes, his voice is soft. He wears white cowboy boots with zippers up the back. A Panama hat with a pink feather. Here he is swept west of the mountain chains, a foggy corner of this nervous republic, and asking me? "Call your damn mama collect!" Ray wishes to shout. Instead he mutters, "I'm not working."

"Neither am I brother!" Howard T. Melville exclaims in a happy falsetto.

"I'm not your brother."

Ray remembers the hustlers and toughs hanging out in the Chicago depot last time he was there, middle of a winter night; men glaring, rolling coin at his feet. Does Howard know the gang that hassled him for money and smokes? "Gotta Kool my man, gotta Kool?" The freezing lakefront, the men busted at the urinals, the trench coat brother dealing dope from an alligator attaché in the ugly Burger King, while Ray waits and waits on the Greyhound to deliver him *please* to the ordered fields of the west.

"Man can you hep me please!" Howard begging now, uncool. The scars put Ray in mind of Little Walter, blowing blues harp, killed in a southside bar brawl, laid low, head kicked in. Reminds Ray of the young ancient faces, the black and white photos on the Chess records. They move uncertainly under the brick of old bordellos and card rooms, posters for the Violent Femmes flapping everywhere. Howard points to the stadium: "Seahawks in there this Sunday or they in Los Angeles?" Now Howard stretches each syllable like rubber, searching for common ground, to be more than a faceless beggar, or a body found rolled in a carpet. "Los Anguh-leez?"

"Hell if I know," spits Ray, preferring the man faceless so Ray is free to loathe him. Howard looks pissed off. Ray worries about offending panhandlers in these times; they're dangerous, shaky about their new calling. You see them hang in doorways, surf music loud as rain on the box, women friends with tracks between toes, under the tongue. That big vein.

Ray craves some eggs *sonora*. What he would give for a hissing T-bone; something with life in it.

"Aw hell. Come on buddy, let's go for a drink."

"Now you're talking," nods Howard under his Panama. He begins singing. *Kansas City. Going to. Kansas City*. They go down some stairs to a table of thick cedar.

"Your health." Ray drinks Rainier. Vitamin R.

"Uh huh," Howard having a glass of harder stuff.

A bearded man joins them. He wears denim, and a red bandana over the top of his head, pirate style. Sunglasses. Ray cannot see his eyes. Keeps trying to.

"Gentlemen," the pirate man says. "I don't take my shirt off in here out of respect for this place, don't show tattoos, I'm an Angel; Oakland, California. Can't show my colours or hundreds of brothers would be here and I'm not talking Gypsy Jokers. Angels! I tell them not to hang around and it hurts me. Jack lets me stow my stuff here, I respect that, but outside on the benches that's my turf, my people, understand and I think you do gentlemen, I'm Eye-talian Irish Indian."

Howard and Ray don't say a word. They drink quickly. The pirate's denim is immaculate. His sheepskin collar is white. His cheeks are smooth, tanned deeply under the glasses.

"Millionaires lock up the washrooms, where you supposed to go? Remember Jack, lights go down and they're gone we're still down here. This is the four corners, a mission on each street, the centre see, the web. . . ."

The pirate struggles for words, points to his palm as a map of the streets around them. His index finger is gone, reminding Ray of the rigs, bits given to the machine.

"It's like a black widow sending lines all over the city from right here! Know what I mean and I think you do gentlemen."

"Yeah sure," say Howard and Ray uneasily. They drink even faster and eye the exit.

"I have seven, hey I have women, but this is different, the brotherhood, the *brotherhood*, IT'S IN THE BLOOD SEE, I'm a Hell's Angel!" The pirate shouts. "I'm Eye-talian Irish Indian! Joliet! Ten years seven months four days. Joliet! Q. Folsom. Nineteen years!"

Tense, Ray studies the bulky man's build and boots, in case he must fight him. It has become ugly. Big dark boots. Howard irritated, his long-awaited drink has turned evil.

"See this is the black window, uh, widow, web, fuck. . . ." The pirate believes he is being deep. Ray stands to leave.

"You want to lay some money down, man?"

"I'm stony," answers Ray.

The ex-con glares with his glasses. "Get away, get outta here!" The pirate stands menacingly. "You people. You see brothers on the road—leave them alone!" he shouts as if Howard and Ray had harassed him, and not the opposite.

"Sure thing," says Ray. They take their empty glasses to the bar and go up some stairs.

"Thought that sucker was going to beat on us," says Howard.

"Nice quiet drink."

"Loony tunes."

"Two-bit extortionist. Wish Joliet would take him back."

"Got to go see a man about a dog." Tide beats in flooded chambers beneath the low streets. Clouds the colour of herons, black evergreens, Scandinavian gloom.

"We see you."

Ray hasn't eaten, has a vision of himself being rolled somewhere, caught with others in the Depression, a post office mural, a Hopper painting, in the USA. *Think positively*, Ray counsels himself. *As what we came for eludes us, so we will replace it. At the food bank there is cheese. Hot coffee and three-bean salad in those cheery church basements!*

Someone passes and Ray sniffs the rich weed. Sensimilla? Maui? Ray peers to the cupped hand, the Pierre Cardins and

V12 Jaguars bought with cocaine, Quaaludes, methamphetamines, methaqualone and real estate, cash in shoeboxes, sultry women waiting in Italian restaurants. A blond! Kissing a neck or fucking a pussy. This is not the fucking Depression. I will not line up for their handouts, gnaw the bureaucrats' cheddar. There is a bone stuck in my throat. I want, I don't know, something.

By brick missions, Chinese grocers, the Merchant's Café, taverns of pickled eggs and yellowed popcorn, Ray walks briskly. A town within a town, copses of bums talking privately, voodoo harmonics. Men with coughs shove at tavern doors; stevedores and loggers and Alaskan fishermen with eye patches and beards, bright socks and metal crutches. No more handouts, vows Ray. He turns twice to see if anyone follows, turns by the South End Steam Baths, drawn to the long piers' cadence of whitecaps and wood pilings, the cranes, trucks' airhorns bleating and men living under the Interstate in a tangle of bottles and sodomy, strangling each other and Ray backs up slowly, the wind cold off the water, backs up to the totem and the souls huddled under the dripping pergola.

Mountains hang in the clouds, pale split ranges each side of the horseshoe inlet, snow dropping this instant into the passes, the white volcano floating at his back, climbers lost up there now as he stares, hidden to each other. At this spot in July 1897, $964,000 in raw gold landed from the north. This must have looked pretty to them, filled with promise. Safe harbour.

Men at the piers plumb the depths for yellowtail, squid. They pass sea-green bottles along the rail. Eagle scouts keep turning up bodies in the riverbank brush. Cormorants hunch like old men on logs broken loose from the booms, moving on winter tides and November storms. A man plays violin expecting change, a hubcap on the walk.

At 4:00 PM the girder crews descend, head home in their helmets, warming Ray with the thought of money made by balancing like gods over the citizens. Ray made as much with the diamond drills and thirty-foot pipe, working the graveyard tower, twenty-one days on, fifty-six hours off. Ray misses the tumult of the drilling floor, pipe hooked on the catline and coming in the V-door, spinning chain, wracking the Kelly back, mud and mosquitoes and black flies, the sweetness of double overtime, of all-night poker. Ray misses the red Buick. A real cock-coach, a leasehand called it. Ray wishes he had his Buick, or even a skeletal moped, streaked with oil. Anything from 1955.

Guitars in a warehouse, the Ramones' *I Wanna Be Sedated*. People in costume cross the square, devils kick pumpkins apart, a weird mist hasn't burnt off all day.

One head bowed while a hand fondles it. Looking for lice? Ray approaches and hears Saved, Jesus, Amen—words like that. The black men draw smirks from those passing in London Fogs and Old Spice. The head lifts and it is Howard T. Melville, trying Jesus on the mainline. His slight smirk says I'll try anything once brother. You know it.

Ray in a room with her in the American Hotel, the view of chimney-pots and roofs and mountains reminding him of northern Europe. She works at the theatre part-time. The irregular patchwork falls to bits under them. Traffic flies past the curtains, lifted on Railroad Way. A glance at sixty-five, her face at the glass. Men fall in the square below as if hit by wind.

"I picked a lot of mushrooms last week. Fell asleep in mushrooms, dreamt of mushrooms." She smiles. "Not those kind of mushrooms." Green eyes. She tries to erase the mist on the window. They are uncomfortable.

"I remember on Halloween, when I was little. My ma always dressed me as a clown. What am I doing down here? Any idiot can do this. I'm pure sick."

She has a small dresser, mirror etched with flowers and tendrils. Walls decorated with pictures of horses and on her nightstand a photo of her father, *The Complete Poems of Thomas Hardy* and an empty can of Coors. On the door a typed list of places to look for work. A Mexican throw rug on the wooden floor, dried flowers standing in a clay vase by the window.

THEY ARE DRAGGING Howard from the Whistling Oyster Tavern.

"What's the charge! What's the charge?"

"No charge. This one's on us."

"DO YOU MIND?" Shoelaces tied to the headboard and footboard.

"Not at all," says Ray. He ties her wrists and ankles. She is naked, face down in the bed, hair at neck, tapering back under his fingers, spine in shadow, skin surrounded by gold and white light, an arm in a shaft of light by the flowers.

"Too tight?"

"No."

The first feel of heat and skin.

"This is a new one to me."

"I need to be touched a while first."

Ray tracing with fingers, his hands around front, learning her long waist, hips flaring, arms and legs to the edge of her bed and then his weight on her lifting.

"That hurt?"

"No, that's nice." Boxcars stumble below, her hard breath driven into the pillow, cock and fingers in her, ear wet in his mouth, biting, the trill in her throat and to Ray a blow, the top seems to explode and he jerks like a fish on a barb, her wet scent and small sparks jumping in hair and nerves. Freed, she raises herself on both arms and takes a long look at him, then drops to the sheets exhausted. Drifting in and out of sleep, Ray half-awake with her breathing on his skin, the small bed, drifting, Ray remembers. Worked this week clearing land on the island, taking the ferry in the morning, chopping cord after cord of alder, now feeling every muscle in her bed, unable to bend his back, stretching, tiny bites on his forearms from the underbrush insects, scratches from blackberry thorns. Money to drink with, day and night coming through like big tides. That last flophouse in Spokane, top drawer, seventy per, the manager Air Force Retired, still going on about the Warren Commission. The grassy knoll, Ray. There had to be another shooter. The manager neglected to introduce his young wife. "Never mind her, breech birth." "I am not," she said, looking at Ray. He asked Ray to sign papers stating alcoholics belong in hospitals, not his hotel. Across from the depot: the Dead End Tavern. Ray thumbed to the coast. To this. Man, I never thought it would be . . . this.

They try to sleep but freeway traffic keeps him awake.

"You eat?" she asks. No.

"I had creamed chicken and rice at the mission. You better take care of yourself," she says. "Have some cranberry juice. Vitamin C."

"I take care of myself. I'm down here but I'm not like the others. I made damn good money on the rigs."

"That's nothing special. I got your number. People don't do this for the fun of it. That Reagan man going on about it, ticks me off something fierce. What is happening to my skin?"

Ray glances at the clock.

"Computers," she says. "That's what I have to get into. Computers are what's what now. My sister in the valley makes thirty-five thousand. What a mess I've made of my life," she says beside him.

There are distant bells and Ray feels steady regret.

"Let's go for a walk," he says. No steeples visible, but bells. Rain on the ocean like flung coins.

"You bet," she says. "Been on all the other rides."

Ray leaves his duffle bag and bedroll in her room.

Under the bridge. 'What's wrong with him?" A head anointed with flies. Newspapers. Pigeons cooing.

"Dead," answers a man over the body, making the word two syllables: "Day-id."

"I have phoned the police," he adds and a number of onlookers disperse. Ray sees Howard T. Melville on the dirt with his head stoved in. His zippered white cowboy boots are gone. The rock by the head. Humming Kansas City.

"You know him," she says. Ray understands. It happens fast and you're alone.

"A drink."

The authorities decide Howard has fallen on the rock.

She kicks through maple leaves and looks at Ray. The clerks sweep the sodden leaves from the walk but next morning there they are, huge wet hands on the pavement, a smell like sardine oil and booze working the neighbourhood. Ray imagines he has children and they are dead. He wants a tribute to what can be hidden, to the sweet conjunction of legs, a nursing student in sensible white shoes, stuffed animals, hammer and tongs, mean head unlocking his jaws and allowing sleep, dreams.

"Old Ed in there will give you a good cut for three."

She walks to the theatre and Ray gets his thinning hair cut by Ed. Here and there the upwardly mobile mix with the palsied heads, the dead-in-the-water winos. The rich rattle on in the bookstore: Herb's flying to DC. The Cultural Committee does not want him to go, his emotional situation is a total mess. "We all had sushi, everything was real strange, oh look at those darling futons!" Art galleries open and close around their whims. Their feet are killing them.

A tall black, in the merchant marine, pokes his head in the door: "Say, do you know the way to the shipyard? This way?" The man drops hash on the barber's floor, a piece from his palm the size and shape of a hockey puck, now rolling on the floor collecting hair. "Going cheap," the man says, chasing it, and he and Ray laugh. "What the hell is that?" asks Ed the barber. The strange Asian green, soft as spring fields. Scissors stopped.

From the square's wet stones a child stares, rock doves crawling his lap in a purple-grey mass, as if feeding from him. His eyes stare from a shirt of birds.

Elsewhere, thinks Ray, kids are getting their good things; Milky Ways and caramels tossed in pillow cases. At The Bread

Of Life Mission men and women line up early, sheepish. *Come Unto Me* spills the neon, like a bar sign. Some lean by the bookstore awnings, pretending they are not poised hungrily for the instant those doors swing at six. They doff hats passing through the door, as if into a country church.

Ray cannot stomach the thought of joining the crowd, entering that narrow portal, mouthing words at the piano.

Ray walks by and she is with someone else. Ray worries he is drinking too much.

"I can control it," the guys say. "Some can't don't you know." They pour another shot down their throat.

Ray sees her at breakfast with a younger guy, joking and whispering over the table. Some older women look at Ray but it is early and he doesn't know what to do; he hasn't brushed his teeth or put on underwear. They stare brazenly at the outline in his cotton trousers. A new age.

Where the Wobblies were shot, where the old sawmill was below the original Skid Road, where the statue of the Indian chief is. The streets that don't meet.

He reads the paper alone, bored, killing time, drinks Irish Breakfast tea, wishing he could think of a way to talk to the women at the other table, instead of waiting for night to start over in darkness, reeling in the gulf of green liquor and the taste of that woman denied to him, mumbling into the cold pay phone, the goddess of thin dimes. Is this the one? How will he know? Breathing slowly and cursing.

"GOT ENOUGH?" asked Howard at the time. "Let's get the juice. What you want for drinking?"

"I used to bring her chink food," the man said. "You know

those little containers. I was driving with the others you know, man I had a red canoe, prettiest little bird dog, things come and go big fuckin' deal right but you know what I've got, you know what I've got and if you don't mister I feel sorry for you."

"Man you got dick you ain't got dick. What a day."

"What are you saying to me?"

"You and me, us and them, what a circus, how much we got man is what I'm saying. Been one hard hard day."

"Don't get my dander. Now is now right, a chance comes by you take it or leave it right? I don't know frankly. Day comes chink food don't cut it and you're drinking with some spade. Did you know her? Where she went? No. You don't."

"Hey I don't know her from Adam, you're not from Chicago, just count up the change and let's get it and get under The Way and kill it alright?"

"Don't patronize me," the man said to Howard. "Here, we got enough coin to do it right. We'll get it done just don't get my fuckin' dander or I'll brain you so help me. Have your guts for garters."

"Ya ya, big talker," said Howard.

RAY IS WALKING. A scabby sidewalk creature, yellow-eyed, hirsute, rises as if from the dead.

"I gave at the office," says Ray.

"You and me," it whispers, "we go way back." It comes on, a partner in a weird contra dance.

Ray pushes at it. Don't come unto me Jack. Ray kicks at the advancing creature. The sole of Ray's Raichle boot splits under the toe. Things are being unglued, now the rain will get in. This places Ray near tears. The thin edge of the wedge.

"Trick or treat," rasps the creature, rolling, tasting pavement block. "Halloween apples," clutching his ragged groin.

Ray runs guiltily. They have forced my hand. Lungs pushing hard. They have driven me around the corner, Ray bounding marble steps to the gas jets and the waitresses' bone structure, the brass breath of the oyster bar, laddered walls of Irish whiskey.

Ray, in a maze of marble, procures New Zealand lager, platters of bay shrimp and salmon on a bed of greens, mussels and clams with julienne vegetables simmered in dry Chablis, butter, garlic and thyme leaves. Fat loaves that scald the tongue.

"How is everything?" his waitress asks.

"Delicious," he replies, both of them smiling. Ray likes her and he is lonely. This is her first week. Last spring she was Miss Missoula. Antelope ate in her yard. Now barristers pinch her, leaving tips and room numbers. Howard T. Melville's ghost and his gang pass outside in their costumes. There is a quarter inch of glass. I know which fork to use, I eat slowly and consider each dish lovingly, I am a real sucker for waitresses. Ray decides he has fallen for Miss Missoula and when he is solvent, when say his blood count is more impressive, he will return to woo her and walk at sunset, comforting each other with tales of their honesty and past suffering and in the flat fields she would pull him down to snap the stalks, mingling his blood with her honeyed skin of apples, her naked ribs floating from the long rope of her backbone. Ray knows he is not being realistic. He pulls the fire alarm.

A golden fat bouncer appears and growls tersely over the shock of bells: "You're a funny kind of duck."

Ray recalls the paycheques squandered in places like this, paying these big men's salary demands. "Correct," he replies and a crowd flies conveniently between them. Ray makes his way to the golden doors, some of the well-heeled stumbling at the steps. A hand at his arm and Ray swings an elbow, feels a tiny nose give way and she drops to the floor, her legs spread wide, ice-blue underthings peeping and blood pouring in ugly syrup from her nose to her lacy blouse.

"Oh no," Ray says, not believing. She peers at the tiles between her stockinged thighs. Jesus now I have hit a woman I have struck a girl, Ray thinks, and the crowd, whitefaced as Herefords, pushes him through the gold doors, firebells clanging above.

In the narrow street the patrons mesh with a larger crowd moving to the stadium with basketball tickets and pennants and children in masks.

Ray strains to peer over heads and sees the fat man lift Miss Missoula from the French tiles, her black skirt high off her legs and his hand pressing her bosom. *Get away from her*, Ray thinks. Her face bleeds crimson into his shoulder. The bouncer glares from left to right and Ray struggles to turn back, to wrest the woman from this lout, from the rainforests and mildewed benches, to go home with her to the heartland, cruising close together in a high PowerGlide, a yard of sweet ozone shaking under the engine on a Great Plains backroad, to eat game hens and steelhead and Saskatoon berries under skies not cloudy all day, to jump in an iron bed at sunset, but no cigar, Ray is accepted by the fat-bellied fans and taken. Another is lost to him. They press like range cattle before a winter storm to the whiskey-coloured dome, the cement breast, the here and now of the sellout crowd, the broker training field glasses on a corn-blond cheerleader, bleacher and hawker, pale mother, lit portal. One is tempted to just keep moving, to drift with the feel of earth underfoot.

He will have to collect his bag and bedroll.

The streets that lead from the harbour: Jefferson, James, Cherry, Columbia, Marion, Madison, Spring, Seneca, University, Union, Pike, and Pine. JCMSUP: Jesus Christ Made Seattle Under Protest.

Geese go south, salmon move on autumn instinct into tributaries. Men and women wander a shore of rubble, lie on seats staring sideways at the blood-black inlet, separate islands, dreaming of an ocean's riches, of Alaska and Asia, sailors' payrolls, trawlers, treasure. Above in the rain and oxygen, sedans blow past without beginning or end.

Ray studies the passengers, balanced on their splashing radials, as if they are from another land. Rosaries knotted around rearviews, staring straight ahead at the river of tin, the rose constellations of tail lights. They lean on fast food, on the Bible, on the horn, burn the fossil fuels Ray drew from the earth. There is no brotherhood. You walk the planet and hammers dance off heads and the women try to cure us at home. *I'm gone motherfucker, you killed me.* Everyone with the same thoughts. *I'm gone sister, I'm gone dinkeyes, I'm gone daddy gone.*

"I'm gone," Ray says, "I'm nowhere."

The road lifts him over the mills and steeples of a Lutheran city, over mouths open in lost hotels of crucifixes and radio tubes glowing like morning planets, over the wild ferns and roses and whores of Pike St. Market.

Night's traffic crosses the roofs, the continent, the century, again and again, on a journey home. No one uses signal lights, they change lanes without warning.

Nowadays Clancy Can't Even Sing

Willie jams the key in the ignition, cranking and cranking the groaning engine. His eyes squeeze in concentration.

"Speak to me baby," he coaxes, chomping on the match stuck in his red face. His burnt nose is peeling.

Hank leans his head on the passenger door window, his cheek flat on the glass, a small shiner smudging the skin under one eye.

"C'mon you whore, start," Willie breathes, almost hissing. Clanking metallically, the purple Pontiac shakes to life. Splinters of harsh light shoot off the chrome. Under Willie's bent fingers the gear-shift quivers, the engine's throb rising and dying and rising, the uneven pulse rattling a loose fender. Hank stares absently at the sun as the pale disk eases into a brown haze.

"Fifty-seven Pontiac," Willie proudly informed Hank the spring afternoon he roared into the dirt driveway, dragging a cloud of blue exhaust. It had rained the night before and the moisture still clung to the new grass.

"Well shit," muttered Hank, circling the car, "Get a load of this."

"Big bulges in the hood like the old Caddies, fit four cases of beer in front of the radiator and the cops out at Pigeon Lake'll never find it." They learned the hard way that this was true only on cooler days, the rad having a tendency to overheat with forty-eight beer blocking any breeze.

Gunning the engine to keep it from stalling. Willie turns to the two girls in the back, stretching his arm along the top of the front seat. "Hang onto your hats gals," he yells fisting the gear-shift into reverse. Skidding out of the parking lot the car swings past the hotel, still in reverse, and careens backwards through a yellow light toward the house he and Hank rent over by Southside Packers. Willie steers with one hand, gripping the suicide knob. A tan leather cover hugs the wheel tightly.

"Takes the miles off," he shrugs by way of explanation to the uninitiated women. Which isn't true, he's driving backwards because he's half-tanked and has coerced some ladies to come home with him from the Egypt Tavern. He's out hogging. Willie seems to fare better than Hank when they go hogging. Hank gets stuck with the dogs.

"What's your names again gals?"

"I'm Marge and this is Yvonne."

"Where ya from?"

"You wouldn't have heard of it," snaps Yvonne who has lipstick on her teeth and reeks of perfume, having added another layer every time she went to the can. Hank rolls his window down to swallow some fresh air. Yvonne seems quite drunk.

She squeals for some disco song on the radio to be turned up. Hank obliges, hating the song, hating Yvonne and her big ass and knowing he's stuck with her and other Yvonnes. "Hey shut the window!" she shrieks, holding her hair down. Hank cranks the glass up. The stench of perfume leaps in his nostrils again.

"Buy cheap, sell dear," intones Willie out of nowhere, presumably referring to cars. "Buy cheap, sell dear," as if Hank and Marge and Yvonne should take notes, the word "dear" sounding strange in the mouth of this red-faced bear clad in a New York Islander hockey sweater and grey sweatpants. This also was untrue, as Willie had yet to sell a single car, dear or otherwise. Every wreck, every ex-taxi, every Galaxie and StratoChief, every Biscayne with turkey-balls and sex-lights, every Chev wahoo wagon missing mufflers and with cracked windshields had been dispatched into one of the solid American Elms that lined the streets of the southside, or were flipped into one of the myriad ditches around the dances at Pigeon Lake or Alberta Beach, lost dodging cops and checkstops or simply in pure heroic joyriding. Two had been towed away over the winter, with dead batteries and square tires, by the police, and were the subject of a number of threatening letters that arrived with some regularity from City Hall. Willie used them to roll huge joints in.

"Buy cheap, sell dear," he insists to Hank and the interchangeable women they somehow cajole to leave smoky dances and taverns, Willie's 6'3" frame squeezed in behind the wheel, steering with one hand, the other tapping time to music or pulling fingers through his sideburns, glancing and smiling at the girls. Hogging, Willie had dubbed it, went hogging

Friday night, he'd tell the boys at work with a grin, Willie went hogging again, lookit the smile on him. Willie squints into the light at the girl, sunsplit grin flashing.

Without fail every Friday afternoon, he breezes in from a sweaty week of roofing with his old man, cracks open a Black Label and flips on an old Buffalo Springfield record or Dave Edmunds' *Here Comes The Weekend*, Willie's rock and roll anthem for this stifling summer. Crunching on toasted cheese and cradling the black phone with beefy tarred hands he enacts the ritual of calling everyone up. Chewing on burnt toast, "What's up?" Invariably very little. Crack open a few more Black Label, roll another number for the road, Neil Young warbling *Nowadays Clancy Can't Even Sing.*

"Hokay hombre," he hollers to Hank from the couch where he lies. "The gods have ordained we go hogging." One end of the frayed couch is supported by a stack of well-stroked Playboys. Willie's jean jacket rolled under his head like a pillow.

"Not this cowboy," says Hank. He clips his nails, snaps punctuating, slivers flicking to the carpet. "I've had it with that crap. I'm going to crack up if I don't get a nice steady woman." Snap, snap. "This goddamn town." In the corner the small black and white is on with no sound.

"No no," counters Willie. "It is written." Willie talks staring at the ceiling, hands clasped behind his head, a Black Label perched on his belly.

"Aw I don't know Willie, the last one was so bad I couldn't get it up.

"Happens to the best of us."

"I don't know. . . ."

"Hey, what's to know?" asks Willie, turning to peer at Hank.

Lucille Ball flickers across the TV screen, her mouth gaping in a silent scream. “I mean, what else is there to do?”

FRIDAY NIGHT, smoke and heat drenching the Egypt Tavern. Gleaming girls sway by the back door, bend over tables in lazy conversation, hazy white light illuminating their hair, masking their features. Bopping madonnas hip-shaking at the jukebox.

“All the same in the dark, kid,” utters Willie, looking straight ahead. Eyes white in brown faces, low necklines and bulging halters, tanned arms bare on the tables, halves of figures draped in shadows, hair lit in blond halos circling faces, tanned skinsheen, white light in the dark, crazy yellow sun splashing in their glasses like beacons. “Tie yourself to the mast.”

The air smells of beer and cigarette butts aging the dirty carpet. With each cold beer Hank’s resolve weakens.

“I still don’t know, Willie.” Weird foggy sunlight spraying through smudged glass, darting shafts of light confusing, disorientating the senses and perceptions, eyes opening up and shutting down trying hard to compensate, adjust, dark wood and chairs, bright dirty glass. Light glares behind bodies, blinding, stare right at them and see no details, no face, a dark outline blazing and black. The broken TV a mute buddha in a high corner of the bar, reflecting the tavern scene, a double, drowning in its encompassing sea-green eye. A police siren howls on Whyte Avenue and Heart rocks and rattles the cheap hotel speakers, the jukebox flickering, heat panting, the Wilson sisters screaming “Let me go crazy on you!!!”

Willie checking out the room, eyes narrowed, thick neck

swivelling, his throat scraped red by the razor. Willie shaves only on Fridays. Humming to the music, chewing hard. A violent rolling motion of the lower jaw, pent energy shoving the skin over the tendons and muscles and bones, slapping his thighs to the fine rock and roll, humming and running his fingers through his sideburns, checking out the action, calculating chances.

"Yes indeed, yes indeed. Will you look at those headlights. Hey, check out these hooters Hank. I'm in love." The shaven hair on his throat and neck bristles, spreading to meet the hair on his chest and head. The side of his face pulses, rolling with frantic chewing, his head cocked to one side, leg shaking and dust-white boot tap-tapping to the jukebox, incessant, on top of it. "Yes indeed." Willie's bulky frame constantly in shorts or sweats, hockey and football jerseys, the names of schools and teams lettered over his chest.

Willie played football in high school but banged up a knee and dislocated his shoulder. The shoulder still pops out on occasion and has to be snapped back in. Now his idea of exercise is to shoot pool. Or, if his latest wreck is running, to lace on a pair of battered adidas, part of his jaded jock look, and tool over to the Corkscrew lounge to watch the Eskimos play on TV. But he likes the clothes, if he has a bad hangover they make him feel vaguely athletic and healthy.

Coffee pots steam by the bar's cash register, surrounded by a legion of Heinz bottles. A pale girl moves through the tavern selling flowers to drunks. Couples are bent over the small tables talking seriously, almost nose to nose. Smoke winds up into the blue-grey light. A blond murmurs, her elbow on the table, cupping her cheek with one hand, the other hand holding her cigarette to her ear, as if she's listening to it. She nods slowly, sensuously, blowing smoke with her pouting lips tensed. She lifts her yellow hair off her shoulders, shaking it a little, and pushes it back. A silk scarf winds around her neck and down over her loose breasts. Hank stares at her for a while and then gets up to go to the can. The floor is soaked with an inch of water and urine. On one wall is a Treasure Chest prophylactic machine, defaced with graffiti.

WILLIE LEANS HIS LANKY FRAME over his parents' cheap pool table. A silver razor blade hangs from a chain strung around his neck. He rapidly smacks the pool balls with a quick scooping motion of the cue so they leap from the felt top. The polished balls arc gracefully through the air of the basement before thudding on the bathroom floor, where they rumble around seeking corners.

"Willie, don't."

Lining up the eight ball he knocks it flying. The black ball rises, hangs in the air and plummets into the open toilet bowl, cracking a good-sized chunk of porcelain from the fixture. Water floods the yellow floor, smothering the rumble of the pool balls on the slanted tile.

"Got it!" cackles Willie, chucking the cue onto the felt. Laughing, he grabs the bottle of Royal Red off the stereo and downs a swig.

Willie's younger sister, Michelle, stands up from the couch and walks to the bathroom. "Jesus Willie, you busted it. You broke the toilet." Hank watches from the Boston rocker, in shadows and light, under the picture windows.

Willie stops laughing and puts the bottle down. "Shut up!

You want the old man to come down?" He picks up the cue from the table.

"Well shit Willie. There's water all over the place." Michelle stands with her hands on her hips, in jean cut-offs, her dark eyes staring at her brother. "And who's going to have to clean the mess up?"

"I said shut up," and Willie whacks her arm hard with the cue.

"Hey c'mon Willie, don't hit your sister."

Willie turns to Hank. "Aw shut up you suckhole. I'll hit her if I want." He stands erect, combing his fingers through his wild thinning hair. "You just wanna get in her pants. You think I don't know?" Laughing, he swallows a sharp swig and clunks the bottle down on an end table. Hank rises from the wooden rocker, grey light behind him.

"I just don't think it's too cool to pick on chicks."

"Zatso?" Willie says over his shoulder. He leans on the cue peering into the bathroom at the water.

"Yeah," Hank replies, trying to keep his voice relaxed. Michelle tosses some towels from the rack onto the water to soak it up. Willie leans the cue in a corner, saunters by Hank and lashes a fist at his face. There is a slight crack and Hank spins back into the rocker, looking surprised and then grasping his nose. Blood seeps between his white fingers. Willie takes another guzzle and trots up the back stairs, two at a time. The screen door slams. A radio breathes softly upstairs and the music curls through the silence left by the ringing of the door.

"Goddamn nose. Bleeds every time I touch it." Michelle carries some scrunched-up toilet paper to Hank.

"Here," she says quietly, glancing at the empty stairs. "Is it okay?" Clutching the toilet paper to his nose, Hank studies Michelle's long legs, the cut-offs' frayed edges white on her brown skin.

"Yeah, I'm okay. Shit, I could live without weekends like this."

"What's with Willie?"

"Beats me, he's been jumpy lately. I think he's into the reds again."

Michelle stares out the window as they speak, the light pretty in her eyes. Her voice is soft. "He's got to settle down." Hank looks at her eyes, bright in the light, at her young face and hair and at her brown legs again, the soft curves of tanned skin under the tight cotton of her T-shirt.

"Jesus." He turns his eyes from Michelle to the floor and then checks the toilet paper. The bleeding seems to have clotted. "Well, you want to head out?"

Michelle rests a hand on Hank's shoulder. "Where to?" Hank feels himself shiver under her touch.

"Uh, I don't care, the bar I guess, where else? What about the water on the floor?"

"Oh," Michelle sighs, thinking more about Willie than Hank or the broken toilet. "Mom'll get it."

THE SUN GILDS the flat street, tinting the air, etching perpendicular buildings, red bricks sharp against a yellow sky. Dust rises where kids in a Beetle spin donuts in the gravel. Windows mirror orange in the strong glare, ragged cloud edges tinged a shade of salmon.

Old ladies in black Dylan sunglasses drag shopping bags,

muttering in Ukrainian, squinting into the sun at Willie and Hank, Marge and Yvonne. The Pontiac noses down the avenue, blurting spumes of smoke.

"The pastel exhaust option." Willie's in shades and a bright yellow R. Angus cap, honking at the office girls off work. Beep beep.

"Stop it you guys, stop it!" Yvonne protests. "Oh gawd, I'm so embarrassed." Honk honk. Willie turns back with his shades glinting sun-silver and flashes a toothy grin at her, still honking. The seats are warm in the sun, the old buildings on Whyte Avenue shine. The car cruises past the dirty junkshops, bookstores, hotels, the Army & Navy, Tracy Starr's strip joint, clunks over the CPR tracks. The Strathcona railroad station is majestic in the light. The car radio blasts. "I CAN'T GET NO . . ." the snare drum ringing, smashing the beat, "SATISFACTION!" They yell along, "BUT I TRY! N'I TRY! N'I TRY! CAN'T GET NO. . . ." Willie sets his hat on Marge's head, the car eases up to a red light and idles, the engine loud and ragged. The interior smells of perfume and Pine Air Freshener.

"C'mon change you whore," Willie mumbles to the lights.

"Hey, watch your language!" crows Yvonne.

"Sorry," grins Willie, "I forgot there's ladies present."

"We're women, not ladies."

"Oh Jesus, the ultimate crime. A thousand pardons."

A woman in a low-cut blouse crosses in front of the car, a string of pearls bouncing over her breasts. Willie wolf-whistles. She reaches the opposite sidewalk and at the bus stop there, a man with hooks instead of hands beckons to her. They talk briefly. He's wearing a lemon-coloured shirt. She unsnaps one pocket flap and fishes out the man's bus fare for him.

Her body is close to his, her fingers brushing his chest to dig out the coins. Hank stares at the woman's brown breasts, the man's silver hooks, the suntanned flesh, the light catching on the metal limbs at the stoic man's sides. Willie's car jerks away from the light, Hank craning his neck at the two.

At the corner past the St. Regis, Marge gets Willie to pull the car over.

"Look, over by the phone booth," points Marge.

"Shit, why bother," groans Willie.

A woman lies on the cement, her feet up on a low concrete barrier, as if she tripped over it and hit her head falling. Hank squeezes himself out of the Pontiac and crosses over.

"Hey. Uh, you okay?" There is some blood on her face. She stirs as Hank nudges her shoulder. She wears a man's jacket.

"Hey. You okay?" She swivels bleary eyes to Hank.

"Fuck off white man." She drops her head back on the cement. Her black hair lies in strings on the ground. Her eyes close. "Fuck off white man."

"Hey, you should at least get out of the open. If the cops see you they'll run you in."

"Hey Hank," Willie yells, "Look in the phone booth, get a load of the dude in the phone booth." Slumped in the booth is a man with a paper bag, his knees hard against the glass. His face is blotched with lumps and boils.

"Jesus H. Christ that's ugly." It looks like he's been vomiting blood. Hank turns away and walks over to the woman on the cement. She snorts and groans, calling out from her troubled rest.

"Hey. C'mon, wake up. Is that guy with you? He looks in bad shape." People hurry by looking at them. "You don't look too hot yourself," Hank mumbles to himself looking at the woman. At the car Willie signals to Hank to come. Hank looks at the two and walks to the car.

"See, I told you not to bother," says Willie. "You run into that all the time up north. Let's go." Marge has moved to the front seat and is hitting the buttons on the radio. Hank climbs in beside Yvonne. The DJ on the radio-news reports a hijacking out at the International. The hijacker, asking for "a world where he can live with dignity" has been termed mentally deranged by the authorities.

At the rented house there are flyers and junk mail stuffed in the mail slot. A Union Jack hangs in the doorway. Willie veers the car right up onto the lawn and gets out, leaving the door open.

WILLIE'S DARK FORM wavers on the boulevard, shoving black hair from his eyes, drunkenly poking his key into the car door.

"Jesus H. Christ, who locked this?" Run-down fences stagger around the yards, battling weed-gorged lots, eerily bleached in the streetlights. Curves of the car are exactly defined, gleaming under the blue bulbs. "OPEN UP YOU SLUT!" he screams, the cry echoing up and down the treed road, the night soaking down. He pounds and kicks the door until it opens, leaving scuff marks in the dust. "Goddamn smokes," he mutters into the black air, taking the pack off the dash, stuffing them into a shirt pocket.

Willie lumbers up the walk, pausing inside the caragana hedge to take a leak. The piss foams, tries to seep into the solid baked earth, around the veined tree roots that struggle out of the cement-like dirt. Stars flower in white fire, Graham Parker blaring on the stereo, howling wind in the black-tooth windows and open door, the Union Jack flapping. Neighbours cringe, crouch behind curtains, telegraphing the hate they have been saving up for their twilight years. Willie sensing it in the air, feeling the venom and laughing, throwing back his head and flashing the famous grin to the street and stars, wide mouth black and laughing. Willie clomps up the wooden porch and pushes the flag aside.

Across the vacant lots surrounding the plant, trucks with stock-racks back up to the Southside Packers' loading docks. The late shift shuffles out to pry the hogs from the now-familiar trucks with boots and electric prods. Willie cracks open a beer in the house. Smelling the blood clinging to the old slaughter-house, the reek of fresh death on the workers, the animals cry through their bristles and dried mud, howl and squeal to the skies, to the moon that washes them in ivory light.

Willie hunches over the mirror, slicing eight lines from the pile of coke, using his silver razor. Two lines each, including Marge and Yvonne, who go to the can together after, to douse themselves with more perfume and blow their noses. Hank writes out a cheque for his and Yvonne's share and trots to the kitchen for more beer. Willie unrolls the dollar bill, taps the powder from it onto the mirror and scrapes it back to the main pile.

"Give me more, give me more," he hums to himself. Marge and Yvonne lie back in the fat armchairs, laughing lightly and listening to *Asleep At The Wheel.* Willie lights a match for a smoke, the flame reflecting in all four beer glasses. Smoke wreathes his face, the sulphur sharp in his nostrils. The ashtray, bottles and glasses sit on an old trunk that serves as a coffee table.

Hank knocks around the kitchen, trying to ignore the squeals that knife across the night, drifting in the hot air that hangs in open windows. Sweat dribbles in his hair. By the back door the garbage bags are starting to smell. The squealing persists. Hank opens the fridge, lit inside by a red bulb. His limbs feel disjointed, a vague pressure rubs at his head. Rushes. Must be stepped on with speed. On the shelves of the fridge are two cases of Black Label, a green jug of orange juice for the morning, a sweaty package of hot dogs and a chunk of mozzarella. Night presses tight on the pink stucco, the heat bled of its light but still grinding. Hank's hearing seems unbelievably fine-tuned, he can make out the TV next door, and unseen in the dark, men cursing the dirty job of moving the hogs. The screams scald the stockyards and slit through the black air above patchy grass and dirt lots, over caragana and honeysuckles and willow scrabbling in the hard earth around the frame bungalows. Hank sips a beer and studies his reflection in the window over the sink. Black all around his face, dark under one eye. Music from the living room drums on, its pulse joining the rush and twist of blood pressuring his arteries, he can feel the bass throbbing, the blood screwing through him. *Speeding*, Hank thinks to himself. Reeling about the kitchen, bent under the weight of various influences, Hank swears he can hear the animals calling him, calling his name. *Goddamn, give me a break.* Hank swerves to the living room.

Yvonne is passed out in her chair, half a beer balanced on the seat's arm. Willie entertains Marge, kneeling at her feet, his hand on her bare legs. Flung back, her plaid skirt reveals white panties with a small red heart stitched on them.

"Queen of Hearts, my goddamn queen of hearts," he keeps repeating while lovingly fondling her, rubbing the white skin inside her thighs. "Goddamn queen of hearts." They're in reverie and laugh like hell when Hank tells them what he heard in the kitchen. Hank can't seem to hear it in the living room.

"Hey, that's great!" Willie spurts between laughs. They crack up on the rug, convulsed. Willie knocks over an ashtray. Hank has to get outside.

"Where's he going to?" Marge asks. She doesn't wear her glasses around guys and has to squint after Hank's disappearing shadow.

"Yeah Hank," Willie sputters, "where ya goin'? Hogging?"

Marge glances at Willie. He fingers her stone-white feet, traces her long toes with red polish on the nails. There is silence and she asks, "What's hogging?"

Willie breaks up, keeps laughing and laughing, giggling between words. "What's hogging . . . ha ha . . . what's . . . hogging . . . ha. . . ." Marge picks up a pack of Craven M, and staring at Willie, lights a smoke. Her silver hoop earrings sparkle, a lamp behind her shining on a glossy poster of Jimi Hendrix. Willie, still laughing, crawls toward her naked legs. She smoothes her skirt back down over her thighs. The ashtray by her hand is crammed with butts, ashes and wadded beer labels. The bass line still pounding, her fingers try to find room to poke one more cigarette in.

THE SALVATION ARMY LADY wanders through The Egypt Tavern. Willie calls her over and puts two quarters in her dry hand.

"Appease your Catholic guilt eh?" says Hank.

"Damn right, it's a good deal. Take it from an ex-altar boy."

Willie's in a blue windbreaker shell. University students argue politics at another table. The waiters cool off in the walk-in fridges, bullshitting amidst stacks of beer cases. The beer at the tables, when you can get it off the lazy slingers, is lukewarm.

"Ah yes, we have used our throats in Egypt." Some old pensioners play shuffleboard against the south wall. No horse collar.

"So your sister's going to school in Calgary eh?"

"Michelle? Yeah, she's gone. She couldn't stand living at home." At the foosball table two players lean over the levers, fat jiggling under their T-shirts. "She's looking for a place to live right now." Willie's hair is squished and straight where his cap rested.

"This place is dead. Let's bomb out to the dance or something."

"Nah," says Hank. His shiner is almost gone now.

"C'mon, let's pick up some cold off-sales and get the hell out of town. Do something different." Willie absently scratches at his chest between the buttons of his shirt.

"Ah, I don't know. I'm sick of it all." Willie stares at Hank for a minute.

"Fuck that shit, I'm taking off." Willie stands up quickly, knocking an empty draught glass over.

Hank watches him leave and sucks back a couple more sips of warm beer. "Tastes like piss," he grumbles to no one in particular, eyeing a man shuffle down the aisle by the bar. Hank remembers Michelle, her brown legs, her hand easy on his shoulder. The man stops, his eyes lowered, face red, and darts down to pluck a butt from the floor. Hank stands up slowly, walks wearily to the front door and outside. Traffic grinds down the avenue. Hank catches Willie's car at the lights. Willie pushes open the door and Hank slides in.

"It is written," Willie says with a grin, fingers tugging at his sideburns. He whips his sunglasses on. The Pontiac chugs into a violent steaming sunset, lavender thunderheads boiling over the lakes, muscled curves to the dark clouds, Hank and Willie envisioning the fast highway west, cruising the dusty backroads. "Look at this whoring traffic." The engine rumbles and shakes, rock pumping the radio. The radios always work if nothing else in Willie's cars. Willie keeps time to *Proud Mary*, bashing his fist on the steering wheel, tapping the gas pedal only on the backbeat, the car jerking and bucking down the sun-slick road. Blue exhaust billows behind. Hank pounds the dash and dust sparkles up from the speaker grille, caught in the sun.

Men Ought Always To Pray And Not To Faint

It has come to this. I must have a cigarette. I hunt around the house, a wet towel wrapping my midriff. A tiny presence itches for nicotine. My heart beats. I shave.

I am not up to dealing with the junkies next door. They lurch like turtles through the dark backrooms or waver white-faced on the stoop, in the heat's smell, their nostrils and mouths moving while they stare, waiting for the synapses to connect, waiting to comprehend.

"A smoke! Do you have a smoke!" I say as if addressing the deaf. It makes me crazy.

I will see if Edna or her daughter Rose is home. Graceful Rose. To watch her undress, finches in the gables between us, in the window her shadowed form undoing silk and blossoms until I am blind as snow. She was the only Rhodes scholar to come from my high school. Now she sings *Darling Save The Last Dance For Me* in the new lounge to the Trans-Canada. I would watch for her on those educational quiz shows, waiting. She jumps decades: one day a sixties Pepsi ad, next day a Cleopatra slut. Saturday night red socks and girlish pedal pushers, Sunday afternoon another century, her legs crossed in sleek boots of dark velvet, pulling at her long purple-black skirt, dark ringlets trembling over an obscene cello: *Elegy*.

I want to fuck her in Montréal but we are just good friends. We climb into deserted prairie stations and neck in the yellow light of empty platforms. Or that night in the summer my truck broke down and I was drunk wandering in the trees. I had a beard like a goat and she hated me.

Her mother Edna sits at her kitchen table with an Indian man the size of a phone booth. The back door is open and I lean in the sill waiting for them to finish an argument. I cannot hear the man, only Edna's slurring words, her voice rough, drifting.

"Who do you think you are? Goddamn mouth as big as your stomach . . . I'm not living with you anymore . . . you want to argue you'll get an argument . . . like hell you're gonna . . . well maybe I decided too."

Seeing me, Edna becomes overly polite. I have income, presence, a driver's license. "Oh come in please. Please sit down. No, I'm sorry, I don't know where Rosie's got to. Cigarettes? Why certainly my dear, help yourself."

Thank God. Lighting up from the blue flames of the gas stovetop I singe a few ends of my hair. I run my hands through it: still damp. It takes time to dry at this length. The other truck-drivers at the freight shed question me about cutting it. They all owe money. The left arm is more tanned than the right.

Driving. I am tired of driving in circles. Dump one trailer and there is another in the Fort McBride door, thirteen forward gears, a flatbed of sod for Calgary, or another load of, say, beach balls and pig iron, another closed circuit of highway. Nothing is ever accomplished, nothing finished, all a trick with mirrors, backing the forty-foot Freuhaufs into place at the loading dock, shimmying riveted monsters into Country Shipping for the pale midnight shift bristling with forklifts and wagons.

I recall every raw-boned dead highway haul, from Iron River, from the barges, from Kalamazoo. Ending in Happy Hour, that perverse moniker.

The Indian's face is pocked from smallpox, his eyes a polished black, a crow's. A blue baseball cap, a thick neck barrelling from his tight windbreaker. His black eyes. The name Raymond Minos is stitched on one sleeve, beneath two lacrosse sticks, crossed, with the script "Saddle Lake Indian Reserve Champs." His nose large, hooked, his hands folded on the table calmly, black veins cording the back of them. Raymond.

Edna appears bent into herself in a ratty hospital bathrobe, her flabby white legs crossed tightly, thick socks to the ankles, and high heels. Her legs are unshaven. Her bony chest is in evidence, close to her thighs as if her body is hinged. Under pointing rhinestone glasses the blue of her eyes is heightened by the bloodshot whites. Edna's hair is dark, matted, with a red-metal tint from hennas, her white scalp visible in places. How is this woman responsible for or related to Rose?

"It's warm."

"It *is* warm!"

"You have anudder smoke dere buddy." His lips hardly moving, his voice more nasal than I expect.

Obediently I have another smoke. We sit smoking in silence. Stacked dishes teeter on the counter.

"Two days I didn't see him," Edna tells me, pointing a fork

in Raymond's direction. I nod, let the tap run until it is cold, not noticing the flow hit a spoon until water is spraying cool over the crotch of my khaki pants. Raymond stares into the stained chartreuse wall.

"Ask him where he's been: you tell me, he says. Ha! If he wants to go out and drink I'm going to get stinking too." She rambles on as if he is not in the room.

"My husband never touched a drop. Lips that touch liquor shall never touch mine, he always said. Now that was a man. . . ."

I can smell her breath. Raymond's eyes and chest are perfectly still. A man, I can't hear him breathe.

"I went travelling with the money," she says. "I went on nice dates," she says. "I paid a dollar seventy for just a hamburg when I's in New York."

"Gosh."

"You ever been to New Orleans? Graceland? Johnny Cash Boulevard? I have."

Raymond pulls one of his boots off and grunting, carves a piece of pungent leather from the inside with a jackknife.

Edna's youngest boy, hardly as high as the stove, begins to fry some sausage.

"Put some eggs on for us honey," says Edna to him, light on the points of her teeth. The boy wears a yellow T-shirt with a picture of Richard Hell & The Voidoids on his chest. It reads "Love Comes In Spurts."

"Nutmeg is good in eggs," says Edna.

"Sure, okay, sounds good. I'll take some nutmeg."

"Don't have none. There's fresh tea dear, you want some tea?"

I wash a mug. Eggs snitter in the cast iron smell of used bacon grease. Voices, smoke in the hot kitchen air. The tea makes me sweat. My eyes do not make out the clock.

"So I says to this New York snot waitress," Edna suddenly jabbing me so I jump nervously. "Just because we had a few drinks in us, just who on earth does she think, who does she think. . . . Hey! I could've done those eggs fifteen times, where are they?" She turns back to me, leaning on an elbow, her cigarette held high and far from her. "Say," she asks, "is that liquor store still open on Twelfth?"

Yes, I tell her. I lean to the sink for water, holding my hair back. The boy puts down our steaming plates. My gratitude is large.

There is never anything to eat at my house, no sustenance. I open the fridge after being on the road and lift heads of lettuce dripping green fluids. I go to the store with fistfuls of money and am lost. The aisles do not have what I look for. I hit the glass doors sweating, with my six-pack and frozen Pop-Tarts. Men, say the women, with clicking noises, absolutely helpless.

Edna shifts her eggs about the plate, her fork tinkling emptily. She swivels toward the open window, yawns, a thread of saliva connecting two silver teeth. I eat the peppered eggs hungrily, drink mug after mug of tea, the hot liquid beneficial as it cuts through my afflicted throat.

The boy snaps open a large Coke from the fridge, pours it fizzing into an A&W mug. He dribbles ketchup over his eggs, slapping and slapping the bottom of the jug with a little fist. Living here, what kind of man will he grow up to be, I wonder.

"Say, is that liquor store still open on Twelfth?" Edna

peering at me again, holding her face up to see through the muddy lenses that have slipped down her nose. *Yes, God yes,* I think.

"I've got some beer if you want. I'll bring it over," I say. Her glasses flash like mica.

OUTSIDE IT HURTS to open my eyes. The pink flamingos still have price tags on them. Heat steams in the road, the moss-backed elms dry, ready to crumble or burst into flame. I am running with sweat and toxins.

My father moved to the north side to labour in the huge diesel shop, trains humping all night inside the grass berms, flowering my childhood dreams with metal, swearing and coupling. I am parched. My mouth forms phrases. I have the beer.

Two approach: styled haircuts and adidas. Ski tags hang from their expensive jackets. One carries a branch from the ravine. This one I offend. He jerks the case from my hand, his blank face at mine, peering as if puzzled, implying "So sue me," the anthem of our society.

I watch a beautiful blue jay glide low under the trees just then. I ask him to return my case. The adolescent swears, the great days of repartee a thing of the past. "Give it back," I insist stupidly. There is something unbalanced about this one, the eyes trouble me.

Fairy, cocksucker, Jesuit, shithead, cheap sonabitch, motherfucker, pedophile. These and other imaginative terms he calls me. Why aren't these two in Europe spending their parents' ill-gotten gains? I don't need this. I reach for my case and his branch arcs at my skull. I intercept it with my left hand and swing my strength into his temple with my right fist. He staggers, knocks the beer case hard into the side of my head and it spins down my back onto the ground.

I return to consciousness on the far side of the street, my hand locked to his collar, smashing the back of his coiffured cranium into a small pin oak, while he stands unresisting, one eye puffy, an unfamiliar grin stamped on the featureless flesh of his face.

I had a fortune cookie the night before that read: "You will attract cultured and artistic people to your home." I could knee this punk, sink fist after aching fist into his moneyed bridgework, but I lack ambition. I let him drop.

A painfully skinny child picks up the branch, chanting happily: "This is my sword, this is my sword!" I pick up the disputed case. A crow wavers overhead against a heel of white sky, in the corner of vision, my head spinning slightly. It must be flaming, as on television, when sunlight refracts, dances as fire on a football helmet.

The inside of my throat: I am reminded of the morning's tête-à-tête with the toilet, lying with it, one hand brushing the cool porcelain, making the usual promises to Jesus about drinking, patches of light playing on the wall, bright as parrot fish. I brushed and brushed my teeth, but still, that taste.

The friend kneels over his buddy, yells something at me. "Be nice," I say. He catches on.

The skinny child whacks a tree: "This is my sword!" The crow stretches wing tips like fingers over the bodies and pink flamingos below; I could use a cool Heineken, some blow; it's Miller time I decide. I am told there is glass in all of us to be guarded. I feel on occasion I am botching the job.

Things should be simple and they're not. I'm a good trucker.

But on the road I want to bring it on home, and home I want to be back at the wheel, moving the world through a windshield like a reel of film. Rose and I talk; she will bug me and ask, why don't I get into another line of work, hire on as a toolpush, go to night school, and I cannot answer her. Is it that simple, I wonder, to rise dripping from the big swamps? I feel pressure but do not know where from. I don't own the right words. Downturn: there's a word. Once I was glee club, Cub Scout and I thought one good deed a day would cover it. That fell away smartly. Just what is a man to do? This fighting bothers me.

Terry, a trucker from Cedar Rapids, says the most dangerous guy is the little southerner. The big guy will fight you straight but the little guy's been whipped on all his life and he'll have a piece. I was daydreaming at the scales and a Peterbilt noses in. Another guy with Mississippi plates, in line behind, climbs out with a gun saying to the Peterbilt, move that rig or be shot. "Aw hell," the guy said and diesel-coughed away from us. Outside Detroit and the big cities the hookers hang out at the Rest Areas, heeling it from truck to truck, twenty-five dollars an hour. Sometimes I lay back and let them work their tired big lip magic. I pretend it's Rosie. I want to be faithful in my fashion, although ex-flames will say otherwise. I pretend she is making her poems with her schooled mouth on my member. It's more than okay. Though I am insecure about visuals, for these women have licked all races and I am not one of these with thirty-eight pounds of dangling death.

RAYMOND MINOS, lacrosse champion, wordlessly pries the caps from the bottles with a spoon. Raymond's hands the colour of an old saddle.

Edna is stretched along the floor, her head resting on a hand. Her second hand touches her cheek, tests the slack flesh, squeezes her own ear, tentatively exploring the whole side of her head. She sees my staring.

"What's eating you driver man?"

"Have a beer driver man," Raymond tells me.

"Sure sure, have some beers till Rosie shows up. And quit brawling in front of my house."

Where is Rosie? I wonder. Could she turn out like Edna?

"Hey Edna, get up." The air refusing to stir, Raymond holding a beer out. Edna takes it, the practised hand of an alcoholic, throws one of her red high heels through the window with her free hand.

"I'm clean!" she yells. Glass tinkles.

"No, thanks, really," I say. "Tell Rose I called by. Hey, and thanks for the smokes and everything."

"Edna, get up. He's going, get off the floor."

"I don't even care anymore," she drones nasally. "I don't even care."

I don't want to know this. As I slip out Edna begins *When The Saints Come Marching In* in an eerie falsetto.

"When that moon turns into blood, when that moon turns into blood, I want to be in that number, when the moon turns into blood!" She's not bad. A second red shoe arcs into the yard, a group of birds scattering and regrouping around it.

"I'm clean!" she shrieks. "I went travelling!" I'm gone.

THESE AIRLESS ROOMS AGAIN. Unable to nap I think of women: my high school sweetheart's breasts, kissing her into coming, to watch Rose cross the yellow grass, cupping an ankle, near tears. Disembodied parts: only one without can fully appreciate these stillborn visions.

The high school sweetheart exited after one too many jealous fights, left me in bed with football on the Panasonic, fumbling with a roll of cash and an elastic, with a vial of black beauties and white crosses. Pale dust on the alleys, dawn and the shadows shifting over the ravine. I stayed on the mattress alone until I had memorized that last disapproving glare of hers, until I could hear perfectly the clicking of her heels in flight over the humming of my own burnt-out drunken grey coils. Until I knew. In the days after I would assemble a sandwich, stare at it, wrap it in plastic and put it away in a cupboard. Her new beau had a big motorcycle, something British. I was sure my heart was going to shake apart into subdivisions.

Rose was married at this time, to another musician, a bass player who worked a day job as a brakeman. I came that close with the high school sweetheart. The singing brakeman swung off into a post and got run over by his own unit. Rose allows that I tuck my shirttails in just like her husband. The sweetheart and I had a couple of reconciliations but she would say the wrong name at delicate moments. Love is a long word; say it with a southern accent, it resonates goofily. "Luv." I like the word "euthanasia," the way it rolls from the tongue like a foreign airline. I dream of the curling rinks of Saskatchewan.

THE RED DIALS AND VU METERS jerk with each power surge, Howling Wolf's deep blues oscillating on the stereo at full volume. A speaker on the toilet seat so I can shout along with *Killing Floor* as I shower. All real pleasure demands decibels: crystal meth out at Skelly's truck stop, V8s, carnal screamers, blasting skeets into powder with an over-under, or a certain Louis Armstrong solo. I need occasional nosebleed levels of life to clear out the cobwebs.

It is in the bathroom that I see I have my mirror Ray-Bans on. All this time. . . . I stare at my visage an inch from the silver glass, every cell in my worn face marked like the skin of a snake. Blind fish intrigue me; never using their eyes in those depths.

The high school sweetheart used tea bags for her eyes, swollen with morning. She slept on her stomach and I tried to take her from behind. She was terrified of conception, and fresh out of condoms, forced me to wrap it in Saran Wrap with an elastic band. You try it.

I lean to the scalding spray, let water stream over me until it is tepid, used. My hands are calloused and slightly burnt from a pup trailer of ice-dissolving compound. It hurts to feather my cock. A shower can be regenerative, a start over in anonymous water. My eyes are closed: back to Sunday roast beef dinners, Yorkshire pudding and gravy in the veins, seeds in the bread, thick pie and yellow custard hot in my throat, grace, sanctuary. Like Edna, I want to be clean.

In the basement's red shadows the air is cool, green light in the bamboo slats, the bricks nearly powder now. Through the window I hear this from the needle freaks.

Rose looks nice, uh, basically well-meaning. . . .

She wants to be seduced by a saint. What a scream.

So pale, the boiled cabbage you know. Or is it punk?

Extreme hairdos.

That trucker, those hick heels . . . what's wrong?

Me? Wow this stuff is better than valium. Wow I'm going to die. Oh I talk too much, just shut me up.

No no. I don't mind.

Sure?

Really!

On the Japanese clock radio Carly Simon sings *These are the good old days*. Outside, a crow is making unsettling sounds. I find the old air gun and fumble brass pellets into it.

The rifle wheezes twice in my arms, sparrows wheeling over yellow lawn. The crow rises untouched, smirking. The needle freaks run and I take good-natured potshots. Teach them to talk.

Again I think on women; their garments, the circles of skin and loose talk. My living room is decorated with lawn furniture pilfered from generous suburbia. My socks are gone. Car thefts are way up. I used to rent rooms to college students but they stole money from my dresser, thinking me too drunk to notice. What I'm driving at is I know I must pay but my pockets are empty. They get you coming and going.

I sift ashes for the longest cigarette end, and light up, dizzy with nicotine. Hank Williams spins 'round and 'round in smaller circles, the needle eating at the black vinyl like a beak. Where are all the women? Cracking at home, a voice answers, sick of the Lazy Leopard Lounge and your ilk.

There are no women in this city, only video games. How is a man to get by, to behave? They want sensitivity but they want you to knock down that pool hall clown who looks sideways at her ass. Well, which is it? It's the doorbell.

Holy Rollers: clean cut, suits erect in the fluttering of sparrows. "There is no man that sinneth not."

"No wait, you young fool," interrupts the older one with sharp hair. "Good morning sir, may we take. . . ."

"Okay fuckers, the truth that leads to eternal life. I want it." They jump as if made familiar with a cattle prod.

"Christ Je-heezuz came into the world to save. . . ." Bellowing between us, slamming of door. "Except ye repent ye shall likewise perish!" yells the younger through the glass, sweat at his face, darkening his evangelist suit under the arms. This decade just started and already it gets old.

A pamphlet lies at my feet. Bold letters: MEN OUGHT ALWAYS TO PRAY AND NOT TO FAINT. I place it tenderly with the mail addressed to Occupant. Across the street a woman in short sleeves drops a lit match to the cottonwood fluff covering her grass. Flames jump and race in a line across the lawn. The woman chuckles, pleased. Her porcine dog yaps and skitters in its circle of silver wire.

I ponder more tea, can I will the arc of blue sparks from kettle prong to wall socket? A football game on the ancient black and white. A distant whistle: vague hulks crash. The black quarterback writhes in pain on the artificial turf, four defensive linesmen towering over his thrashing, sheepish at trying to kill him seconds earlier. "This crowd's giving him a big hand, Dick." The black man is loaded into the darkness of the old ambulance. "Yes Dick, these are grrreat fans of the game!" On the next play the fullback's knee blows apart with an audible crack. "There are no flags on the play."

If I close my eyes, I hear the rhythmic chant and roar of the crowd as a swish of huge wings. I envy birds' flight, even if only migratory loops. I change channels and a glove connects in slow motion, driving a wet mouthpiece and what appear to be teeth into space over the judges. I ask for little: a lull in theatrics, decent salsa, a car that starts in the winter, the girl next door. They give me Tampax ads and ritual violence, speed traps, disco. It is hot. I will combust. The men seeking payment, the encyclopedia salesmen and evangelists, the hawkers, parasites and junkies, these will steal in my house to find ashes on the divan. Other creatures must live in the high growth of my yard with the birds. What becomes of them when the Public Works men arrive with writs and equipment to cut back the errant yard?

"Yoo-hoo!"

Rose is in the hall in a green bikini. My gun and a towel in her arms. "Is this yours? I found it on the sidewalk." Today the look is *Beach Blanket Bingo*. "Here."

"I was defending your honour. How have you been?"

"So-so. When did you get back?" We circle each other, not talking of what may be on our minds. "I had to get out of that madhouse," she says. She turns the TV down. She puts a hand to her ear and I recognize Edna's gesture. "Could I use your bath? Edna says I have been off with men and the modern diseases and cannot use the family tub. It's just a hair too depressing." Her eyes on mine, stepping out of the two green circles, eyes on mine, her hands meeting modestly, the nervous stepping motion burnt into my mind. I rise, I close the door, slam the birds from the mountain ash, a ball of the feathered scattering in an odd curve like a school of fish.

ROSE IS BURIED UNDER MY COVERS, as if trying to hide.

"Is it time to get up?"

"No, you can sleep," I answer. 9:24 AM. I'm up unusually early, giddy because of her presence. I will not lose this. I will settle down for her, be guilty of conspicuous consumption, drive all night for her, circles or no circles. I will buy vegetables, things may work out. No. I will lose her, because I want her too much I will lose her.

Showered, I crawl back into bed and work my fingers through her hair. "You feel cool," she says sleepily, "you feel cool." Once more we lift the birds from the trees. My heart beats. I hold her and I hold her.

Goose, Dog, Fish, Stars

There are black antlers, cashews, a clock made of pool balls. "You should meet Olofson," the young bartender says after a while. His eyes dark, the skin around them unmarked.

"Why not," says Hank.

Olofson wears a bleached work shirt, has a bit of a beard, weather-beaten cheeks. He looks to Hank like a longshoreman, maybe a sailor. Second generation Swede, raised by the docks of dark Ballard. "Give me something that will sneak up on me," calls Olofson. "Leave me handicapped." He waves a muscular arm around. The bartender pulls down a bottle of bourbon: Fighting Cock, the label says.

"This is basically nutritious," he offers solemnly.

Olofson nods, pale eyes closed, head moving like a blind man's. Behind them the coast guard pilots shoot eightball.

"Don't I know you from somewhere?" speaks someone.

"I don't know," Hank says softly.

"This tastes terrible!" Olofson the sailor cries, eyes still closed, drinking it anyway. "Well, how do you like it here?"

"It's interesting," Hank says. Locals seem disappointed by his replies. Is he to kiss the ground every ten minutes? Hank thinks of the frigates that once called here, holds heavy with stone ballast, timber, or the silk trade. He wonders if Virginia is sleeping. They had argued earlier about a guy she had slept with in Wyoming.

"She's bummed," grumbles one of the pilots at the tables. "Hasn't talked to me since I had that Cat run into the side of her trailer."

"Sure. Why not," his partner answers, studying the lay of the balls. A woman shrieks in a distant booth.

"Never did find that marriage certificate. Got the dee-vorce papers though. Those I need!"

At 2:00 AM the doors are locked but Hank and Olofson drink on, the bartender drawing them Red Hook gratis. The bartender reaches in a yellow box of Hav-A-Tampa jewels, lights up a bomber and passes it across the bar to Hank. "What the hell," Hank says, and has a toke. He imagines telling Virginia about it in their motel room.

"No clams this year," says the bartender in his smoke.

"Dead as doornails," says Olofson the sailor. "Took a backhoe to the beach. Zero. Nada."

"Oh," says Hank, feeling somehow to blame.

"Are you working right now?" they ask. The lights are dim, Los Lobos plays manic Tex-Mex accordion on the cassette deck.

"No. Not working." What had he been thinking of? Virginia. He feels sudden affection for her.

"It's bad right now."

"What is this stuff? Paint thinner?" asks Olofson, examining the bottle of Fighting Cock. "I think I've been damaged," he says holding his chest. He stares sadly at Hank.

"But you, you're both working?" asks Hank.

"Well, you know." They glance at each other. "This and that."

The joint is strong. It is cut with something, it makes itself known. Olofson lectures on about loss of the clamming season to the peninsula, about blackmouth salmon, about money or *chickie-pull* as he terms it, and about his dogpack theory of human behaviour.

"Think about it," Olofson the sailor says. "Like dogs. It explains everything. Even the clams."

Dogpack theory, I'll have to remember this, thinks Hank. The bartender touches his dark moustache.

"This one knows what we're talking about," Olofson says, nodding sagely. "Right? We're not rabble. Not everyone knows what we know." They study Hank.

It seems profound. Hank comes to believe that Olofson is the devil, in Port Angeles to talk personally with Hank about his dogpack theories. Hank is laughing and there are arrows in him: he is pinned to the bar at the knees and elbows. He is St. Sebastian. Deer and antelope play. He is in his white pants. They keep staring.

"He liked that joint now, didn't he?" says Olofson the sailor. "I'm getting definite vibes from this one. He knows what's what." The accordion wheezes to a halt, pale air hanging.

Hank realizes they are after his ass. The handsome bartender and the grizzled sailor. They have the wrong man, he tells them. He can't stop laughing but the boys don't find it so funny. "Why me," asks Hank. There was another, a dull servant with a broom. He pointed out Hank as sympathetic, likely, alone. And Hank stayed late with them, taking their drinks and smoke. Olofson flexes his biceps.

"Did you hear the one about the goose?" Olofson asks the bartender, pointedly not looking at Hank. "Seems there was two guys, want this same goose. In the tussle the goose got its head smashed in." His voice has anger in its edges.

"Gotta go," Hank says. "Don't like the parable," Hank says.

"He's gotta go," says the grizzled sailor to the bartender. "I guess he's not going to get physical." He seems disappointed. Hank finds the door.

"Watch yourself," says the bartender at the top of the iron stairs. "And whatever you do, don't say you're sorry. They all do."

Hank descends into the black alley. The door closes above. He walks warily to the front of the building, expecting cocks and knives under the skein of stars. He climbs up and crosses at the sidewalk. A dog howls by the quiet mill.

A black and white pulls out of the darkness of Front Street. For a moment Hank is relieved to see it. ID, says the policeman. Hank has none. "If you'll take me by my motel, I can show you ID."

The policeman runs his fingers over Hank's legs and torso. Hank gets in the back. He thinks about police shows on TV. This is not really happening. The plexiglass slams into place between them.

"Can we talk through this," Hank pointing at it, an odd echo with his words now.

"Yes, go ahead." Hank realizes the cop feels a confession is forthcoming.

"No, just wondering, you know." Hank has been drinking

since the afternoon. It is now 3:00 AM. Plus the joint. Things go around but he gets hold of it. The cop mutters at his hand. The radio crackles a reply.

"Why you interested in me?"

"Burglary. Not ten minutes ago. You fit the bill. Where you been?" The spine of the road bends.

"That bar."

"Closed an hour ago," counters the cop. Hank is wary of mentioning the two in the bar. Some alibi. He wonders about the two men: did they want to fuck him, or want him to fuck them? Just what is the etiquette?

"I know you from somewhere. Any record?"

"Speeding tickets, you know."

The tires hum uphill. The officer wears no hat. Hank studies the back of his head, his ears. Off in the distance squares change to triangles; the pull of perspective. Gravity pulls at Hank's face.

AT THE FLAGSTONE, Hank steps inside to find the wallet in his other pants. Cheap-Eddie is asleep in his bed. Virginia is awake, hugs Hank.

"Where were you?" she asks. "I was about to call the police." Hank laughs at this, tries to explain what has happened. He cannot stop laughing or slow his babble. He feels basically he is crashing wings, bull in china.

Outside with the police, Hank articulates slowly, politely. Like two different people, Virginia tells him later. In the light of the parking lot Hank shows his Canadian passport, driver's license.

"You smoke?" they ask.

"What, marijuana?" Hank asks, trying to sound innocent. Is this a set-up engineered in revenge by the sailor and bartender?

"Come on. Tobacco."

"No. No. I don't smoke," relieved it is not about dope. A second patrol car bumps into the lot, carrying a woman and a man in the backseat. Their apartment had been broken into. They woke to see the burglar. A black policeman walks them past as Hank speaks with the first officer.

"Yes, that's him," they say.

The officers inform Hank that his age, build, beard and dark T-shirt all match the description. "You have the wrong man," Hank insists, as he had to the men in the tavern. This is getting old. Hank talks and talks with them, giving them Virginia's California plate numbers, their IDs, various numbers, names, addresses, cities.

"I'm convinced," says one uniform finally, the black man. Which way? wonders Hank, what does that mean? And then they leave, leave him to go inside the room with Virginia. Cheap-Eddie has slept through it, dreaming of pieces of silver.

"I'll never sleep after that," Hank groans, lying beside Virginia.

"Talk to me," she says.

"What about?" Hank says.

"Talk to me," she says.

Hank passes out. She lifts and drops his arm several times but he is gone into whatever it is.

THERE IS BANGING. "What the hell?" mutters Cheap-Eddie, blinking like a mole in his blankets. Hank opens the door. Two badges are held up. The older detective in a shiny suit that is hard on the eyes this early. "You want to get dressed and we'll talk," they say. The mountains look pretty behind them.

Hank pulls on loose pants and a shirt, talks with them on the hood of Virginia's MG. Sunlight glares off every plane. Hank feels at a disadvantage; he is pale, shaky, unrested. The detectives have showered, had their coffee and breakfast.

"I know you from somewhere," one says. "You play ball?" Virginia brings a glass of water. Hank is touched.

"I talked with the police last night. You have the wrong guy."

"We'd like to hear it again."

The plainclothes seem to look down on the uniforms. The B & E artist has done any number of jobs and they want to nail him so badly you can smell it. Hank will do in a pinch. They want him downtown.

The older one in the golden suit tries to come on tough. They have probable cause, he says. He has a lot of laugh lines and his hair is greased straight back. He reminds Hank of a TV preacher. Or he played a guitar in say, the Ventures. The younger detective is blown dry, in a tasteful sienna suit. He seems apologetic and looks like someone Hank used to know. It will come to him. Hank's head feels a turn too tight. And what will the neighbours think?

"Can we see that purse," the older one pointing inside the MG. Of course it matches the one stolen, down to a lipstick smudge.

"Been in Port Angeles before, Hank?"

Now Hank feels the MG's California plates seem suspicious,

as does the heavy flashlight given Virginia by a worried brother in San Diego. As do the tools in the trunk, ditto the tire iron, Hank's socks, anything. They get to you, thinks Hank. They say you did it, then you did it.

The detective rifles the purse, inspects Virginia's bank book. The gold suit shimmers.

"They can't do that," she says to Hank. They do what they want, thinks Hank. The veils drop lickety-split. Things become evident.

"Are you working, Hank?"

"No sir."

"Not working huh."

They take Hank to the ghost car. "Call my brother," Hank says to Virginia. Cheap-Eddie has not shown his face for fear it may cost him. "Call my brother in Victoria."

Hank is in the front seat this trip. They back onto the highway, the older detective at the wheel. How easily it happens, and what the hell is probable cause, wonders Hank. I was weaned in the suburbs: aren't I exempt from all of this?

"You keep your mouth shut some of the time. I like that a real lot," the older detective says, as if reading Hank's mind.

Farther west the street is blocked off for the annual salmon derby parade. There is a naked woman at a window. There are barricades and bowlegged Kwakiutl and Quillayute Indians wandering booths of beargrass baskets. Dogs run in circles.

"You smoke, Hank?"

"No. You have the wrong guy."

"They all say that. No offense or anything. Last week it was a woodcutter slit a hobo's throat along the river. Same deal."

The ghost car pulls in an alley and Hank assumes he's going to get roughed up. The older one walks with his head bowed to a dumpster, peers in it, spits or tosses something, Hank cannot tell. Looking for evidence? Planting it?

"What's he doing?" asks the younger detective from the back.

"You're asking me?"

"This'll get him." He slips his pistol from a shoulder holster, levels the gun at the window and shoots it at the older detective. Hank jumps, his stomach paining him.

"Goddamit," yells the older man, "you firing those blanks off again? You didn't shoot it at him did you? Jesus."

"I was just showing him," says the younger detective sheepishly.

"Well we have to account for every goddamn shell or the chief will have our ass in a sling. Every shell!" The older man fumbles in a small box, then throws the box at the man in the back seat. "The numbers better be kosher my man, or your ass is grass." He slams the car into gear, mumbling.

They back out of the alley fast and drive the one-way downtown. Snow-touched mountains move behind the brick buildings, reminding Hank of Wyoming, of infidelity. He can imagine the face she would make when he put it to her. Some stranger.

"Been fingerprinted before, Hank?"

"Yessir, with the railroad. You have a computer, right? Can't you feed me in and see if I'm clean?"

"Only works if what you're giving us is straight."

"Did you know this is the world's largest fishing derby?" asks the younger detective. "Really super prizes."

"Whatever happened with that big blond tart?" the other asks.

"Oh her. She discredited her testimony, no one believed a word. But I got a great deal on her Nova. With the divorce she's selling everything, going to Alaska, get away from it all."

"Well I tell you Anchorage is dog meat," says the older man. "Bumper to bumper with all the new cars and money but nowhere to go. Terrible place for the family. Dog eat dog I tell you."

This can't be happening, decides Hank. He begins a gloomy meditation on chance, the greased passage from wrong place, wrong time, to shit creek and lack of paddle. If only he'd left the bar five minutes earlier, if only Virginia hadn't gone back to the Flagstone in a huff, if only he'd quit school in grade eight and gone into Real Estate. The real felon is likely in a sunny kitchen nook, forking up scrambled eggs and reading of his latest exploits. Hank feels peckish.

"I should at least get a breakfast voucher or something out of all this.

"Not from us," says the older man, grave as a fish.

Hank turns his eyes from the men and the mountains to the Strait of Juan de Fuca, past the tottering canneries and coast guard buildings, hears the thumping of a freighter clearing Ediz Hook, watches oystercatchers and curlews trot in the surf. Slime-green waves run in one after the other. One sneaks farther; the others follow. Dogpack theory. A heron seizes something in its dagger bill.

Hank understands this beautiful country has been made ugly for him.

He thinks of the couples moving on the sunburnt tides off

Tongue Point, Cape Flattery; with their hooks and coolers of ice, searching for the main chance, the trophy salmon, the happy coincidence of bait to unsuspecting prey.

He thinks of the mix of currents and creatures, the pieces of the food chain. And over that sparkling blue stripe is Canada, the leafed islands just out of reach. Hank wishes to climb in a sloop with Virginia, drop the keel and become a dot on the horizon.

They lead him from the ghost car and he may as well be guilty for the way it looks. Tongues rattle, daughters drawn to fat mothers. A murmur of drums; the Port Angeles Rough Riders Marching Band and Color Guard bleats, prances in the parking lot, warming up for the big parade. Dragoon hats, tiny fishscale skirts in light and legs, bosoms and thighs lifting to the sun. Batons hang forever. Much of life here seems to involve parking lots, understands Hank.

Flags full of stars droop everywhere. *I hate marching bands*, Hank realizes.

Inside the building few uniforms lift their heads. Another wayward one, no big deal. They talk, laugh at a joke about Dolly Parton.

"I'm cutting out for coffee," says the older one to the younger detective. "You finish up here, alright Jimbo?"

Hank is fingerprinted in the hall. A man brushes his teeth at the water fountain.

"Sorry if my hands are cold," says the little woman in a uniform of blouse and skirt. "Some of them say my hands are cold."

She rolls black ink on a glass surface, takes Hank's hand in hers. Each finger and thumb is rolled in ink and pressed to the paper forms, to the squares.

"Sorry dear, let's try your thumbs again. I can't seem to get them right. See?" She shows him the flawed impressions.

"Sweaty palms?" says the young detective. He rubs his palms together, then holds out a trembling hand, in imitation of a nervous prisoner. The detective is grinning. *A joke*, realizes Hank, *a joke*.

"Let's try again dear." She grabs his thumb.

Beyond the walls the band begins its anthem. Tuneless horns blat obscenely and drumbeats push hard through the blond wood of the hallway. Now the thing is starting.

Afterword

These stories were written by another person, they were written by me in my twenties, between 1977 and 1983, when I was moving between Edmonton, Victoria, and Iowa City. They were finished in Seattle in an attic in the U District and in the basement of the Elliott Bay Book Company down in Pioneer Square, the bookstore where my girlfriend the poet Sharon McCartney worked at the time.

All of the stories kindle addled memories for me of that lost life, but I think the story "Cowboys Inc." was the most important to me, was a watershed for my approach to writing. There are stories here that I wrote before "Cowboys Inc.," and stories I wrote after "Cowboys Inc.," and I can tell which are which.

I wrote "Cowboys Inc." while at the Iowa Writers' Workshop; I lived in a wrecked house that cost me fifty dollars a month and I worked with Bharati Mukherjee, Clark Blaise, Barry Hannah and the late poet Larry Levis, and in Iowa City I met Ray Carver. I had driven numerous road trips through the

Dakotas and Colorado and Wyoming and Montana and Idaho en route to the west coast and Alberta, and back to Iowa and Chicago, and I had a shoebox of notes, matchbooks, cocktail napkins, maps, scraps, beer coasters, and postcards. I wanted to write a road piece, I wanted a triangle, and I wanted to make use of a guy I worked with as a janitor, a guy who popped speed and was always ready to punch someone. I also wanted a dead man as a character, and I wanted a sex scene on an ironing board (the ironing board was not biographical; I never iron).

Usually I would try to make a story as smooth as possible, work on every word and segue. Some earlier stories took forty drafts. But "Cowboys Inc." quickly hit a point where I had an early draft, albeit a draft with jagged edges. The story wasn't easy to digest, was not A to B, and not tied up with a pretty bow, but I realized I liked it that way. It had the power of pastiche or collage, a quality that was accidental and brutal, but attractive to my eye and ear.

I felt I had stumbled onto something evocative, broken through to a new way for me to smash together matters of head and heart. Not everyone agreed, some reviewers said to skip that story and read the others, but I was happy with it.

My next book was the hockey novel, *Salvage King Ya!* It took a hell of a long time, more than I could have ever known. I started the novel at Yaddo, the writing colony in upstate New York, while also working on this collection. In the novel I hoped to find a middle ground between the later form and the earlier more traditional stories in the collection.

Back in Alberta, Rudy Wiebe told me he was surprised how *tough* my collection was; I couldn't see that effect at the time, perhaps because I'd written each story separately and didn't think of the impact of them gathered together. But at the time I was very much influenced by writers such as Hubert Selby, Celine, Bukowski and even Raymond Chandler. I assumed hard-boiled stories were better than boring stories set in a coffee shop, and I had yet to assimilate Cheever, an idol of mine and a writer who made it damn clear that suburbia and family could be excellent material.

This collection won the Writers Guild of Alberta's award for short fiction, but, just my luck, there was no cash prize at that time. The prize money kicked in the very next year. I wouldn't protest a retroactive payment if Alberta has a few extra dollars kicking around the vaults, or I'd accept shares in the oil sands.

I read that Flannery O'Connor used to laugh out loud reading her own stuff and I like that. It's funny to look at these pieces again, funny strange and funny ha ha.

I laugh at the premise of "That's How Strong My Love Is." My friend and editor Sharon Sterling once complained that all my stories were set in bars, so I decided to write a new story with the character *not* drinking. Where does the character end up? In a bar nursing ginger ale instead of lager. That story's original title was "Hockey Night in Canada," but I had an old song stuck in my head while walking Lower Muscatine Avenue in Iowa City: "That's How Strong My Love Is" became the new slightly tongue-in-cheek title.

I laugh at some of the dialogue in these scenes. When I first started writing I could not write dialogue. When I drove a truck for the railroad I stopped at every hole-in-the-wall used bookstore searching for old Chandler books with lurid 1940s covers and for plays to help me with dialogue. I had no ear and reading playwrights forced me to concentrate more on what people said. My freight shed was knocked down and those tiny used bookstores all disappeared and I didn't notice.

I laugh thinking of my Harry Truman era electric typewriter down in my parents' basement. The thing was round as a turtle and so heavy I could barely move it, but I miss that hulking monster humming under my hands like a vigorous vibrator. I bought the typewriter from a used business equipment store in Edmonton and soon found that it threw the letter E every few minutes, threw the metal letter in the air right across my bedroom. I taped the E down but it would slowly work loose from the straitjacket of Scotch tape. On the white page the E's imprint would climb higher and higher than the other letters in the same sentence, as if mimicking musical notes in a melody of its own making. And then into space flew the E again.

I used that monstrous typewriter for years, but when I first made a bit of money from writing I bought a bigger dictionary and I bought an early laptop; no more metal letters flying across the basement room.

I miss those youthful days of flying metal, but I don't want to travel back to that basement on 132nd Street or the dead end jobs or the constant rejection letters nor do I want to travel back to the jail in the Port Angeles, Washington police station.

I was picked up by the police in Port Angeles, as described in "Goose, Dog, Fish, Stars." For months afterwards in Seattle I jumped visibly when there was knock at the door or a police cruiser in the rearview; I kept thinking they were coming back to get me, to drag me in one more time.

That time passed. It is much more pleasant to have these stories come up again in the rearview. My thanks to Ruth Linka and Lee Shedden for this new edition, and thanks to Sharon Sterling and Ellen Godfrey and Dave Godfrey for wanting to publish my stories in the first place.

Mark Jarman
Fredericton, NB

Other Books by Mark Anthony Jarman

Ireland's Eye (Travels) 2002
19 Knives (Stories) 2000
New Orleans is Sinking (Stories) 1998
Salvage King Ya! (Novel) 1997
Ounce of Cure (Editor) 1992
Killing the Swan (Poetry) 1986
Dancing Nightly in the Tavern (Stories) 1984
Nothing North of Disneyland (chapbook)
Surfer Joe Among the Fishes (chapbook)
Dangle (chapbook)

Mark Anthony Jarman is the author of *19 Knives*, *New Orleans Is Sinking*, and the travel book *Ireland's Eye*. His hockey novel, *Salvage King Ya!*, is on Amazon.ca's list of 50 Essential Canadian Books and the number one book on Amazon's list of best hockey fiction. He has been short-listed for the O. Henry Prize and Best American Essays, he won a Gold National Magazine Award in non-fiction, has twice won the Maclean-Hunter Endowment Award, and has been included in *The Journey Prize Anthology* and *Best Canadian Stories*. He attended the Iowa Writers' Workshop, has taught at the University of Victoria, the Banff Centre for the Arts, and now teaches at the University of New Brunswick, where he is fiction editor of *The Fiddlehead*.